OWNED

HIGHEST BIDDER

WILLOW WINTERS

LAUREN LANDISH

OWNED: HIGHEST BIDDER

BY LAUREN LANDISH & WILLOW WINTERS

She thought this was a game. She thought she could walk away.
She thought wrong.

I've lived a cold, unforgiving life. I've seen things, I've done things, that would break a man. If they didn't kill him first.

With my past behind me, I have nothing. No way to atone for my sins and nothing to lift me from the depths of despair I've come from. And no one to give me the control that I so desperately desire.

But as soon as I saw Lilly walk through the halls of Club X, something inside my cold heart flickered. With her large, blue eyes, and her seductive curves, I wanted her. Lilly, my flower. There's a sweet innocence about her that steals the breath from my lungs. She brings my darkness to the surface, and what's more… she craves it just as much as I do.

The danger is what lured her to me. But she didn't realize how intense this would be when she signed that contract.

She thought it was all fantasy and make-believe. But I'm not a knight in shining armor. I'm not a hero from a romance novel. I'm the villain.

And now she wants to leave?

I won't allow it.

I own her. And I'm not letting her go.

Owned is a Dark romance. A full-length standalone novel with an HEA and no cheating.

Want more? Join our mailing list to receive bonus deleted scenes! (If you're already on our lists, you'll get this automatically).

PROLOGUE

Joseph

I'm quiet as I walk into my bedroom, hoping to get a look at Lilly without her knowing. But those doe-eyed baby blues are shining back at me the second I enter.

Hating me. They pierce into me, giving me a look that could kill a lesser man.

I've been given more hateful glares. From deadly men who intended on killing me, who despise me and my very existence. I've never been affected.

But the look in her eyes guts me.

Because I know she's hiding pain behind the hate.

"Let me out," she says in a low voice as she wraps her fingers around the silver steel bars. Her voice lacks the strength and conviction she'd rather I hear. She adjusts slightly, and as she does she winces. My eyes follow her movements; the grates of the cage have left an imprint on her knees. It's only been a few hours since she's been given her punishment. And I'm already regretting it.

I have to remind myself that this is for her own good. She's being punished for a reason.

She *wanted* this.

She *asked* for this.

And now she wants to leave?

I won't allow it.

My hands ball into fists as I stalk forward, my bare feet sinking into the lush carpet with each heavy step. The cage is large, much taller than her own height, and she rises to meet me although she remains on her knees.

Here's a side to her I've never seen before. The fierce woman who was always there, hiding behind the facade of obedient eyes.

She liked to *play* the submissive. She thought this was a game.

She thought wrong.

Lilly looks back at me with daggers in her eyes as I crouch lower, leveling my gaze with hers. Even with the anger swirling in her blue eyes piercing into me, she gives off an air of purity, of innocence. She's so delicate, so sweet. *My flower.*

Her rage only makes me want her more.

"Are you ready to *obey*?" I ask her, tilting my head slightly. My words piss her off. And I fucking love it. The comprehension of her predicament makes her eyes narrow for a moment. I watch as her hands attempt to ball into fists, but she corrects herself, warring between what she craves to do and what she feels she's expected to do.

She clenches her teeth, but her eyes water. Tears form in her eyes as her lush lips part, but then quickly close without a sound being uttered.

I question everything in that small moment.

"Fuck you," she finally responds with a sneer, but then instantly lowers her gaze. She's strong, courageous even, but she's a true Submissive. I have yet to earn that side of her. But I will.

"You want to," I answer with a sharp smirk that curves my lips up, and that brings her glare back. We're at an impasse. If she'd give in, so would I, but she's fighting it.

She didn't realize how intense this would be when she signed that contract giving her freedom over to me. Neither did I.

She doesn't respond, but I see her thighs clench ever so slightly. The small action makes my dick instantly harden with desire. She loves what I do to her. She still wants me, even when she hates me.

"All you need to do is obey, my flower." I regain my strict composure, waiting for her answer.

My nickname for her makes her lips part just the tiniest bit with lust. It makes me lean into her that much closer. Wanting more. My fingers wrap around the bars just above hers, barely touching her, but feeling the heated tingle I always do when I'm with her.

She knew I wasn't a good man.

That's part of what drew her to me. I know it is.

"Fine," she says in a mere whisper. I cock a brow at her answer, daring her to continue with that disrespectful attitude.

Our days are numbered, and if I let her, she may leave me the moment she can and never look back.

But she craved this arrangement for a reason. The same darkness that drives my desires is also in her. Stirring low in the pit of her stomach, fueling her hatred for me, but making her want me so much more.

"You know that's not the way I'd like you to address me."

"Yes, sir," she says obediently, her voice the proper tone as she squares her shoulders. She's still eye level with me, and there's still a fierceness to her, but she's willing to play. *That's just how I want her.*

I'll show her how good this can be.

But first, she needs to be truly punished. The cage door opens slightly with a gentle creak. I need to leave a lasting impression.

She may be angry with me, but she's still mine.

I *own* her. And I'm not letting her go.

CHAPTER 1

Lilly

"What in the effin' hell?" I slam *Playback*, the romance paperback I'd been reading closed with an angry growl. My blood is boiling like an evil witch's cauldron.

"How could it end... like *that*?" I grit my teeth, shaking my head at the gall of whoever's written this. I fell in love with this storyline, and totally felt the heartache and brutal pain the hero and heroine went through. I was rooting for Liam and Tilda. Their story gripped my heart from the very first page, and I was quickly drawn into their struggles to overcome the heartbreaking obstacles keeping them apart.

I'd read each page breathlessly, flipping through the book like a hungry wolf in search of his next meal, practically dying to find out how it all ended, and then... I gulp as my throat constricts into a ball of tight anger, unable to understand how someone could be so cruel. I'd invested so much of myself into the story, hoping to be rewarded with a satisfying conclusion to such a tragic relationship.

Then it ended abruptly. Just like that, with no happily ever after, no resolution. Only a tragic heartbreak that left me feeling raw. I can't believe how completely engrossed I was in the book, feeling like I was part of the characters' lives, only to be shafted at the very end.

Burning up with anger, I turn the book over and peer at the binding, determined to commit the author's name to memory so I can make sure to stay clear of reading any more of their future work. *Lauren Winters.* "More like Slutty Winters," I mutter angrily, feeling thoroughly cheated.

I know it's fiction and it's not real, but I hate when I get emotionally invested in characters and then something like this happens. It makes me feel absolutely cheated.

I groan my frustration, tossing the book on the end table. My eyes are drawn to the roaring flames of the marble fireplace in front of me. The heat of the fire pricks my already heated cheeks, and I relax slightly as I'm enveloped by cozy warmth. Despite my sour moment, I *love* this.

It's one of my favorite pastimes during the cold winter months, sitting in front of a roaring fire with a hot mug of coffee and burying my nose into an engrossing romance novel. I just like it better when it's a book that doesn't leave me feeling like my heart's been ripped out of my chest and stomped on in front of me.

"I need something more mindless and smutty after that," I mutter, picking up my cup of coffee and taking a sip. I'm calm now, but I still have a slight urge to toss the book into the flames. I must admit the author did a good job with everything else. I just didn't like her ending.

I just wish I hadn't stepped on my Kindle. I had like fifty awesome books piled up on my to-be-read list.

Sighing, I get up from my cushioned recliner with the

book in my hands and stretch out my limbs, several of my bones popping as I stand. But it feels so good, I hold the position, letting my limbs come back to life.

My eyes take in my living room, and my mood lifts again slightly. It feels so homey in my new townhouse, especially with how cold it is outside. I've decorated it with warm earth tones that make me feel right at home. The walls are lined with decorative shelves that are filled with books. I've read every single one of these books. A few of them are even autographed.

I love my new bookends, too. They're pale blue mice carved from stone stone to look like they're holding the books up. Just seeing them makes me smile.

This room is completely mine, and finally feels like a home. I still have the rest of the rented townhouse to put my stamp on, but this one room is just perfect. I walk to the large window across the room to open the curtains and let the evening light in. I can feel the cold from the winter air coming through.

Outside, I can still see confetti lining the streets from the New Year's Parade as I place my hand against the window. It's a few days past the first of January, and a few pieces are still blowing along the edges of the building.

I grin as I take it all in, the ending of the book quickly forgotten. I could write a romance that would leave me with feelings that would brighten my day. It's okay to make my heart hurt a little, but I don't want it broken. That's not why I read romance novels.

I've actually had a very good year, albeit a long one. I just finished my next-to-last semester at North University and I've passed all my classes with a B or better. I even managed to get a B+ in Advanced Calculus, something that's always been a struggle for me, all while working hard as a guidance counselor with troubled students at a local high school. I will never understand why psychology students have to know calculus. At this point, I just want to graduate and start giving back by helping make a brighter future for others as a teaching counselor in the local youth detention center. It's their last chance before their delinquency sends them beyond public schools and straight to jail. It's not a job I take lightly.

I can't handle the high school kids though. That's for damn sure. For this past paid counseling internship, the program threw me in a classroom with twenty students. I'm only twenty-four and petite, so even on my best days, I hardly look over twenty-one. To say the students didn't take me seriously doesn't even begin to cover it. I cannot handle working with older teenagers. At all. Sure as hell not twenty of them at once.

Some of those kids got under my skin so bad that I thought I was about to have a stroke. It takes a lot to get me worked up and thinking negatively. But I found it difficult to stay positive as the semester progressed. I still managed to persevere though; a few students showed so much improvement, and I know I made a positive difference in their lives. In the end, that's all that matters.

That internship is over, thank God. Next year, I'll be in a middle school and that's where I really want to work. I feel like I could do the most help there.

And now I have the entire winter break to catch up on all the romance books I've neglected as reward for my hard work.

I glare balefully at the book in my hand, thinking, *I just need to make sure I don't read any more disasters like this one.*

Huffing out another small sigh, I walk over to my bookshelf and pause before I slip the book back into its spot. I really should toss the damn thing into the fire. I'll probably never read it again. In fact, I know I won't. But I can't bring myself to do it. Books are my biggest obsession; even ones I don't love. They keep me sane and positive. They give me hope.

It's time to get dressed and move on. I love my book boyfriends and getting lost in romances, but I have other plans tonight.

My body crackling with excitement, I put the book back on the shelf and make my way to my bedroom. I'm going to Club X tonight, a place that literally embodies the BDSM fantasy elements I love reading about. It's a fantasy come to life, and I freaking love it. It's been my secret pleasure for a while now, and I'm having a blast just showing up and observing the BDSM lifestyle. From the rich, powerful men, to the beautiful and willing sex slaves, and the hot and heavy playrooms with wild, untamed sex—it's all so incredible. I suck in a breath as heat burns my cheeks, and my nipples pebble at the thought. The experience has been so much more liberating and intoxicating than I thought it would be. Even if I haven't actually participated yet.

It's exactly the place I need to be to research the themes I'm putting in my romance novel that I've been writing on my downtime while at school. The book isn't anything I'm taking too seriously, and I don't expect for it to ever be published or seen by anyone else's eyes but mine. I just love writing the stories that come to me. It's a stress-relieving outlet I enjoy indulging in, especially when I've had a particularly bad day.

I walk into my bedroom, tingling with excitement, and dig out a beautiful red nightgown out of my closet. I bought it just for tonight. There's a PJ theme tonight at Club X, and I don't want to be sent home for breaking club protocols. I set it down onto the bed, running my fingers along the soft silk fabric, thrilling at how luxurious it feels.

My skin pricks as I stare at it. I hope I'll look beautiful in this tonight. Just thinking about the looks I'll get from those powerful, handsome masked men causes my breath to quicken, and my pussy to clench. A fiery blush comes to my cheeks, a little bit ashamed at how turned on I am. I don't engage with them though. I stick to the safety of the trainers. I'm not ready for this to truly be real.

I can't imagine how people at school would react if they knew I was attending a place like Club X. A twinge of worry pricks my chest at the thought. I don't want anyone finding out, and I'm filled with anxiety every time I show up at school after a night at Club X. I worry that someone will recognize me and out me. But with how strict the rules are at the club, and the non-disclosure agreements that have to be signed just to get through the doors, I let the worry slip by.

I'm still slightly shocked about how I found out about it. Or rather, *who* told me about it. One of the teachers at the high school I work at, Mrs. Nicole Flite, mentioned the place to me after she saw me with my nose stuck in an erotic romance novel over lunch break. She was cautious at first, probably scared that I would look down on her or rat her out to the principal when she told me about the darker elements of the club. But when she saw how intrigued I was by the whole thing, she let loose, filling me in on all the exotic details.

I couldn't believe that a teacher who looked as sweet and unassuming as her could even be part of such a dark, sexual world like that. But then again... so am I. And now I'm hooked. This place embodies what I've been dreaming about after reading my romance novels.

It took a lot of work to build up the courage for me just to go. But I finally did, and I don't regret it at all.

I still haven't seen Nicole there yet in the weeks I've been going. And I'm not sure I will. From what I know, she's married with kids and she doesn't get the chance to go often anymore.

I haven't been able to go that much either, occupied with school and work. Only on the weekends during this past semester.

But now that I have all this free time over the winter break, I'm going to make the most of it.

I slip the red nightgown into my bag, feeling the adrenaline rush through my blood, and walk out of my bedroom, intent on spending a night lost in fantasy.

CHAPTER 2

Joseph

J bring the whiskey to my lips, taking a swig and then wiping my mouth with the back of my hand.

The amber liquid warms my chest with a vicious burn on the way down. I revel in the feeling. I need it just to feel at this point. My life is devoid of anything meaningful to me. I have wealth, I gave up power, and now I'm alone.

I made the right decision though. I left the *familia*, taking the fall to get the heat off their backs. But now I have nothing, and no one. I'm bored, and that's what's pissing me off the most.

It's better than taking over the familia though. Even if that does make me an outcast.

I clench and unclench my hands into fists. My knuckles are sore from boxing earlier today. I spend most of my time in the gym in my basement. It's all I do at this point, workout and survive each day. Just like the prisoner I am. Caged within a prison of my own making.

I don't fit in anywhere. Like the fucking Beast in his

castle. I huff a humorless laugh, swirling the whiskey in the glass before taking another swig. I can feel the warmth flowing through every bit of me, coursing through my blood and finally giving me the buzz I was after.

I want to drown in this feeling. I need it just to sleep. The visions of what they've done and the blood still on my hands burn into me when I close my eyes.

I killed them. I helped eliminate those thieving, lying murderous bastards. Not for revenge, not for a righteous vindication. Killing the Romanos was a message. One that the community and our business partners heard loud and clear.

But someone had to take the fall for it, and I was eager to leave. I don't want to be a monster. I don't want a life of corruption and pain. It's a ruthless lifestyle. But it's the one I was born into.

I stare down at the worn leather journal in my lap. I'm writing every memory down as they come to me. Partly for documenting it, partly to relive it. It's fucked up that I'm trapped by the memory of a world I was so eager to leave, but the sins of my past refuse to let me move on. And I don't know why yet.

I close the journal and run my finger along the stamped name on the front. Passerotto. *Little sparrow.*

But that's not my name. It's what my mother called me. And this journal is all I have left from her, save a few dark memories.

Joe Levi. Murderer. Villain.

That's the only name I go by now.

I'm sure this wasn't what my mother imagined this journal would be used for, but she's buried six feet under in the cold hard dirt. I down the whiskey at the thought.

I was raised to be ruthless and cold, brought up in an environment that breeds sick fucks, like my own father.

13

They think I'm corrupt or maybe even a snitch 'cause the charges got dropped. The ones I was meant to take the fall for, but they don't know how or why they got dropped. Some think I have more power than I do, which is helpful at times. I'm still feared, which is better than having a target on my back, but it leaves me lonely.

The fire crackles in the large den. I stare at the logs, the fire spilling from the splits between the wood. The back of the brick firebox is black with soot.

I enjoy their fear. I need it to continue to survive. What's worse is that it breathes life into me.

I didn't have a choice.

Lies! The voices in my head sneer at me. They hiss that I could have done more.

They all should have died. My father, my brother.

I shouldn't have stopped at just the Romanos.

I set the empty glass down and lean forward, my head in my hands and my elbows on my knees.

I've done horrible things. I didn't have to. I chose to, so I could survive. So I didn't have to run my entire life with the threat of death hanging over my head. But I still didn't have to do it. And now the memories haunt me.

My phone pings on the end table, drawing my attention and breaking the repetitive thoughts that I can never escape.

I slowly reach for it. There are only three people it could be. I dread the ones from my *familia*. They can all go fuck off. But they don't seem to get the message. I read the name on the lit screen, and relief and something else flow through me. Comfort.

Kiersten. Or Madam Lynn, as she likes to be called nowadays.

She reminds me of the one good thing I ever did. The whiskey pales in comparison to the warmth that memory brings to my chest.

They left her for dead. But I helped him save her.

It wasn't enough for all my sins to be forgiven, for all my wrongs to be righted, but I'm proud that she's still here, even if he isn't.

She's a close friend and nothing more. It's only recently that I've begun to leave this house, and it's all because of her. She's always talking about how she owes me; she has no idea how wrong she is. There's no doubt in my mind that I'm the one who owes her.

She wants to help me, but she can't. I'm beyond repair, and there's nothing I want from her. It's a sweet gesture that she tries to fill my dark days with *something*.

I rub the sleep from my eyes. It feels late in the dimly lit room with the thick drapes closed, but the darkness is just setting in beyond the walls of this house. This prison I keep myself in willingly.

Are you coming tonight?

I read her text message and debate on my answer.

I have sinful fantasies, some a product of the way I was raised, but others I've grown to desire of my own accord. I've yet to give in to the impulse driving me to keep going to Club X. It's alluring and intoxicating in its nature. The atmosphere is a heady mix of sex and power; so intense, it alone is a drug.

Just last week I bid on a Slave at her auction in Club X. I'm not a fan of the term, I prefer pet, but neither really matters.

I've never paid for sex before. It's not about the money at the auctions, it's about the contract. About getting exactly what I want, and ensuring the lines are clearly drawn and everything is written in black and white. Everything consensual. ...even if its nature is not.

That bid wasn't a bid for pleasure. Although she made me

curious, I didn't want her. Her Master called her Katia, his kitten.

I thought Isaac was humiliating her, making her go onto a stage knowing no one else would bid on her. Making her feel undesired. I know the man, and I know what he's capable of.

I was pissed. How could he treat her like that? She was trembling on the stage, her apprehension and fear apparent. I wanted to make him pay for what he was doing. And steal his kitten, set her free even.

But I was wrong.

I don't understand them, the members of the club and the elite circles who have grown comfortable there. This lifestyle is new to me.

But control isn't. Sex isn't.

Power is in my blood.

My phone pings again. I don't want to read it. She always convinces me to go. Maybe it's because I feel for her and what she's going through, but I'm not interested in playing games and trying to fit in where I don't belong.

I toss the journal and pen onto the end table and rise from my seat, feeling my muscles groan with a pain I find pleasurable. I take a peek at my phone in my hand when the reminder ding goes off.

Kiersten's text reads:

She's going to be there.

I stare at it, thinking about the one thing that's interested me in the last three years of living in this void. I ran into her when I left the last auction. Literally. I ran straight into her small, delicate frame and nearly knocked her over. I wasn't paying attention. It was my fault entirely.

But she took the blame.

Kneeling, improperly, and apologizing in a hushed voice.

She was perfectly imperfect. In need of a Master. But not

yet accepting of one. She's still learning. Kiersten caught on to my interest when I started coming to the club more often.

I've been watching her. I needed to observe her.

She has desires I'm not sure I can fill. The way she craves pain is something that feeds a monster lurking inside of me. A depraved beast I've tried to keep chained.

I should stay far away from her. But she piques my curiosity, and she's made me truly desire her. Or at least I crave hearing those soft moans and forcing them from her lips myself.

I've watched her closely this past month. I'm not sure she's noticed. No one pays her much attention since she's still finding her limits. She's not eager for a partner either. She sticks with the trainers and stays in the shadows and corners, keeping out of sight.

I can't deny that she tempts me to possess her, to teach her proper techniques. I tap my fingers on the wooden end table rhythmically as I consider going tonight.

I picture the curve of her ass as she practices her poses, the way her lips part with lust when she touches herself discreetly. She may think no one's noticed her, but I have. And I want her.

I text Kiersten back, *I'll be there.*

CHAPTER 3

Lilly

I WALK up to the doors of Club X, the huge mansion-like structure looming in the background, its red ambient lighting illuminating the front of the building and casting a glow on its esteemed guests that are waiting to be admitted. A cool breeze blows through the area. My skin pricks as the air softly caresses my flesh, crackling with electricity, and the dark-suited bodyguard at the door recognizes me.

His eyes trail the skimpy outfit I'm wearing, the red silk short nightgown I changed into before getting out of my Honda. I feel almost naked under his gaze, but at the same time incredibly sexy; he makes me feel wanted. Although the attraction is firmly one-sided.

I should be used to this now, but I still get nervous with anticipation. I know that in a few moments, men far more powerful than him will be looking at me, and it makes me feel anxious. Unconsciously, I trail my finger along my bracelet. It's rubber without any metal rings, meaning I'm still just learning. I haven't yet chosen a membership bracelet that will indicate what I want in a partner, Dominant or Master, or someone who enjoys the more painful side of BDSM. I'm afraid to admit that I'm still a virgin, although there's a bracelet for that. I would rather have a Submissive or Slave bracelet, although I'm not sure which one yet. The lines are blurred for me still. And I'm not sure how much control I'm really willing to give up. The fantasy of being completely at someone else's mercy makes me weak with desire. But the reality has an entirely different effect. I think the aspects of pleasure and pain are what intrigue me most. I haven't felt the sting of a whip yet. But I really want to. I crave it like a sweet-toothed freak fiending for their next Twinkie. I just haven't asked for it. It's as easy as letting a trainer know that I'm ready. But I haven't taken the plunge yet.

Deep down, I know that actually committing to it is going to take a lot. So right now, I'm just observing. It's all just research for my book. Or so I tell myself.

I'm admitted through the doors by the dark-gazed body-guard, and as I step into the club I have to suck in a breath. I've been here a lot, at least half a dozen times, but I'm still floored every single time I walk in. Club X is beyond beautiful with thick lush carpet, extravagant furniture, gorgeous ambient lighting and soft, tantalizing music that makes my blood heat.

But the thing that gets me the most is the very air that surrounds the people.

The men who walk the floors of the club radiate power and wealth beyond imagine, and the women who follow them are too beautiful for words. I watch as a masked man pulls his timid partner along by a gleaming silver chain, his eyes filled with determination and swirling with lust. I keep my gaze safely away, knowing it's not my place to look a Master or Dominant directly in his eyes unless I want to draw his ire. I'm supposed to be Submissive, and acting anything otherwise will get me in trouble. Even if I'm only here to watch. I can't ruin the fantasy that Club X provides so perfectly.

I shiver as the atmosphere of the club seems to wrap around my body, my nipples pebbling. I love this place. It's even better than reading my books, and that says a lot.

My lungs fill with a deep, steadying breath, as I try to get control over my emotions. It's almost as if I've taken a hit of a powerful drug and I'm getting high. That's what this place does to you. It gets you high on lust, power... sex.

I lean against the bar just past the foyer and breathe in deeply, cooling my heated blood.

I know I want to go to the dungeon, but first, I think I need a drink. It's dark down there, and I'm not sure I can handle it without at first numbing a part of myself. I need to free my inhibitions.

As I wait for the bartender, I glance across the large hall. The stage on the back wall is dark tonight, with the curtains closed, and I don't know if that's a good thing. I look forward to the shows, since not only are they exhilarating, they're a great learning experience. I order a shot of tequila, making sure to keep my gaze in a safe place. Within seconds, the shot glass is placed in front of me by a beautiful bar vixen with long dark hair, wearing the same professional uniform the other employees have on. There's no mixing up who's working here, and who's here for play.

The liquid burns as it goes down my throat, but it's a comfortable feeling. I know it will help me deal with the experience of the dungeon. Even though I'm hungry for it, the alcohol aids me in handling the intense sexual emotions that run through my body. The alcohol is nothing in comparison to how intoxicating the sights in the dungeon can be. I bite into the lime and let it wash the taste of the liquor out of my mouth, the sourness making my eyes close tightly.

When I'm done with my drink, the fiery liquid warming my belly, I leave the bar and make my way through the halls, blending in and trying to disappear amongst the crowd.

A few men approach me as I pass the playrooms. I swallow thickly, my heartbeat racing as I pause in my steps. I don't look at them, but I make sure that my bracelet is in view. Once they see it, they move on. No one seems interested in someone who still doesn't know what they want.

With the rubber bracelet on my wrist, the only people who talk to me are Submissives waiting for their partners, or the trainers. I like it that way. It makes me want to keep the bracelet forever. It makes me feel safe. But the days are limited. The membership here is expensive. Too fucking expensive. The first month with this bracelet was on the house. Madam Lynn, the owner I think, said that I could stay to see if it suited me. But next month I have to pay up if I'm not paired up. And I'm not sure I'm ready for that. Or if I ever will be. But the month is almost up.

It's hard not to stop and stare at the sexual acts taking place in the playrooms as I pass them. The men and women going at each other with untamed depravity. Their moans and cries and grunts and groans assault my ears, the smacks of their flesh pounding against each other filling my already heated blood with sexual desire.

I ignore it as best I can, although my breathing is coming in faster, and continue on into the darkened corridors, my pulse racing with excitement.

There's nothing in this world like the place I'm about to enter. The playrooms are an intense experience, but down here it's far more... primal, possessive. Raw in every sense of the word. I make my way down a dim hallway to where two men dressed in dark suits wait on either side of a large iron cast door. They're employees, guards who make sure that everything runs smoothly. And that no laws are broken. They give me a cursory glance before opening the door, the sound of its creaking making my heart jump in my chest.

I take in a ragged breath before I walk into a dark stairwell, the only lighting being small, glowing red sconces on the wall, giving the area an almost evil feel. A few masked men pass me on my way down and their way up, their dark gazes holding secrets that chill my blood. One man even stops to look at me as if thinking that I am looking to be taken, but when he sees my bracelet, he keeps moving like the men back at the playrooms.

They respect that I'm not ready, and not a single person has tried to push me. There are rules to the club, and they're strictly followed. It makes me feel safe. It's odd to think that way, given the nature of this place. But I do feel safe.

I shudder to even think about what goes on through the heads of the Masters and Dominants when they look at me. It arouses me in a thrilling and exciting way. A way that hardens my nipples, and sends a pulsing need to my clit. I'm almost ashamed at how turned on I am by their questioning glances and piercing stares, and the sinful thoughts I know are lurking behind their eyes.

It's just like how I imagine things in my books. I only hope I can write about this in a way that does this place justice. A way that captures the sensual seductive side along with the other emotions coursing through my blood.

As I get closer to my destination, a shrill scream that's a mix of pleasure and pain rips through the stairwell. It's followed by whimpers and moans. I pause, gripping onto the banister for support, my breath stalling in my lungs. I've been here many times, but I still can't prepare myself for some of the darker things that happen in the dungeon. It's so sexually intense that I become dizzy with desire and emotion. Thank God I've taken that hit of tequila. After I calm myself, I continue on until I make it to the bottom floor. The sounds of groans and seductive pleading fill my ears. It's a place that resembles a seventeenth century English dungeon, with cages and racks on either side of the room, and lit torches along the walls. The ambiance is everything that makes this room... it's all so tempting and forbidden, mixed with danger and fright.

It's more private here, especially this early, but I've seen many things here I never imagined I would. Things that have turned me on. Scenes I've watched play out, and then later been ashamed to have gotten aroused by. I've seen a woman beaten with a whip until tears were falling down her cheeks, her ass bright red from the lashes. But she leaned into it. She begged for more. Her Master gave her what he felt she needed, and the way he took her after made me desire the same ruthless touch.

I want to feel what she felt. I want to experience it to understand why she desired it as much as she did.

I watch, stalking along the edges of the room, as a naked, dark-haired woman is bound to a bench. The rough rope is coarse and would chafe her skin, but her masked Master places a thin piece of silk under it. Her lips part in a soft mix of moan and whimper as he binds her so tightly she can barely move. I can see his huge hard cock pressing against his silk slacks. It forces an intense wave of arousal through every part of me.

The Master, or Dominant, I'm not sure, is wearing the membership bracelet. His rubber bracelet is joined by two interlocking metal bands of silver, and in the center, a red band. I shiver at what the bracelet signifies. This dude is into some dark shit. Sadism and Masochism.

I've seen this couple before, though I don't know their

names. I don't know anyone's real name, actually, other than Nicole. It's funny--I've been coming here for a while, and I don't know anything about anyone. But it doesn't bother me. I'm here for the experience. And names are rarely used inside Club X.

Another couple is seated on a bench, and I've seen them before, too. The man gives me chills like no other. And not in a good way. His eyes are beady, and pure black. His hand is gripping his pet's shoulder, squeezing. He's always touching her, or pulling her collar. I've never seen them interact in any way other than what they're currently doing. She's on her knees on the ground, looking straight ahead and he's behind her, whispering into her ear.

Her hair is wispy and unkempt, which also makes them stand out. None of the others look like her. They're taken care of in ways she's not. Most of the women here are given looks of jealousy from me; I can't help it. But not her. I can't help the sympathy I feel for her.

Of all the people here, he's the only one that doesn't seem to belong. And it's all because of the way he treats her. The way she doesn't beg him for more. The way his touch seems to wilt her spirit, rather than enhance it.

I rip my eyes away from them, hating that they're here. I have to ignore them whenever they come down to the dungeon. Instead I focus on the couple in the center of the room, the reason most everyone is in this room. The ideal couple. The one that exemplifies what I consider to be the fantasy of this lifestyle. I watch as he kisses her softly on the lips and places a blindfold over her eyes. There's a guard to the right of them, watching vigilantly. There's another one stationed at the end of the room, also watching the couple and the onlookers like me. These men observe every detail. They see everything. The men in the suits are here to enforce order in case things go too far. They know the safe words ahead of time. Although everything is done discreetly. And some couples don't use safe words at all.

I was shocked the first time I saw one of these men disrupt a session. I could understand why though, because the woman was screaming for her partner to stop. The very fact that the guard felt the need to step in made me fear for the Submissive. The guard merely stepped forward and requested that the Submissive give her safe word. The Dominant stepped back immediately, lowering the paddle he was using on her, and the Submissive gave it, out of breath and still writhing in the binds that held her down. She whispered the word green and then looked to her Dominant, waiting for more. I got the feeling it wasn't the first time a guard had interrupted them.

The man in the suit stepped back, and the scene continued. The Submissive kept screaming as her Dominant fucked her ruthlessly, using her body mercilessly, fucking her with vicious need and smacking the paddle against her skin as he took her almost like a caveman from prehistoric times.

It was a rape fantasy reenacted before my very eyes. It was very difficult to watch, and my eyes kept going over to the guard that was standing nearby. But he didn't move again. As long as the Submissive didn't say the safe word, the Dominant had complete control over her. They were free to act out whatever fantasies they shared in complete safety.

For couples without safe words, they merely nod at the guards when asked if they're alright. Or so I've been told. I've only seen a guard interrupt once. I'm surprised how many couples don't have safe words. Some simply use 'stop'. I suppose it's different for every partnership.

Most of the clients in here seem paired up, like these two. It makes me envy them. Especially when they're collared. Collars are like wedding bands. My eyes fall to the floor, and my heart thuds. Maybe that's more of my romance novels slipping in. I don't know for sure that the people here regard collars so highly.

It's hard not to confuse reality and fantasy. But that's easy to do here. This place is like a fantasy come to life.

A movement out of the corner of my eye causes me to look around. The breath stills in my throat, and my heart skips a beat. There *he* is. Looking at him, I can hardly stand, my knees are so weak. He's like a dark prince, dressed all in black with his matching half mask, the edges of it looking torn. It only serves to enhance his chiseled features. My breath quickens as his eyes bore into me with an intensity that makes my skin prick. The room seems to bow to him. Everything urges me to bend to his will. *And I want to.*

My heart pounds rapidly in my chest as I stare at the floor. A chill travels down my shoulder and through my spine. He has a power over me more intense than anyone else. A pull to him so strong I nearly give in and fall to my knees as I feel his gaze on me.

I've seen this man before. In fact, I ran into him when I was new to the club. My cheeks burn at the memory, remembering his dark regard of me, the flush of my skin as I sank to my knees and apologized for being so clumsy. He watches me sometimes when I come into the club, and I'm always almost overwhelmed. At first I thought it was all in my head that he was checking me out, and then I thought I was just getting carried away by my fantasies. But he followed me down here.

He must want something from me. The thought makes my body come alive with desire.

Or maybe it really is all in my head, I think to myself. No one knows me here. I've tried my best to make myself as invisible as possible.

But as I move away and walk over to the Saint Andrew's

Cross that sits next to a rack of whips and rope, I can feel him following me, stalking my every move.

My breathing quickens as I do something new. I slowly fall into a kneel, trying to remember every detail one of the trainers showed me about proper posture. I can't believe I'm about to do this. But my body feels compelled by a mysterious force.

I show him submission.

I invite him to have power over me.

CHAPTER 4

Joseph

I CAN'T TAKE my eyes off of her. It happens every time she comes in here. *Lilly.* I follow her, staying a safe distance away, her gorgeous curves stringing me along. I'll never admit to her how much power she has over me; I can't help but follow her through the club, watching her and gauging her reaction to the variety of kinks. I know she's seen me this time.

She's not put off by it. She doesn't seem frightened, although I obviously affect her. It's as if she's waiting for me. She's never done this before. She's never invited anyone into her personal space. Let alone kneel as though she's been waiting for me, offering me a chance at her submission.

Seeing her kneeling there, looking vulnerable and sexy as fuck in that red nightie makes my cock harden, my heart beat faster. I take a quick glance around the room, a possessive side of me rising from deep within my veins, but no one moves to go to her. A few eyes are on me, narrowing with questioning looks, but they fall when I look their way.

I ignore them all. I always do.

They don't know shit about me. And I give zero fucks about what they *think* they know.

These masks are good for hiding the identities of the men from the Submissives. But it's no secret who we are to one another. The tight social circles that run this city, both from the highest highs of skyscrapers and penthouses, to the dirtiest lows of the pulses that run the streets—are all infamous in their own way. We all know each other. We know who has business with who, and what side each of us is on. Right now, I belong to neither, but I'm well-known to both.

I can tell from the way they look at me out of the corner of their eyes without moving an inch, without even breathing. By the way they stay away and avoid me at all costs. I know for a fact that they *know* who I am. And I sure as fuck know who they are.

We're all powerful men here, and with too much to lose to engage in this kind of activity around people we don't know. Even with contracts and NDAs, we're bred not to trust. With so far to fall and so much to lose, most of these men stay in the private rooms once they've found someone to pursue and indulge in.

But me? I have nothing to lose. And I know exactly what I want. Or rather *whom* I want.

I approach her slowly, almost cautiously, as if moving too quickly will frighten her away. The very notion that she's offering this gift to me, thrills me.

She's been coming to the dungeon more often as if she's looking for something, as if she needs some kind of depravity that she can only find here. But she's yet to engage with anyone. That's what I've been waiting for. For that moment when she's ready to test how her pleasure reacts to pain, and how much freedom she'd get by giving over control.

It piqued my interest to see desire flash in her eyes when she watched the tails of the whip hit against the soft skin of a Submissive. She wasn't frightened by it. She was intrigued. She was *aroused*. She hasn't experienced the pain yet. I have no idea if she'll actually enjoy it.

But I'm excited to find out. The anticipation clouds my judgment, and makes me focus solely on her.

The guards in the room are watching over the other couple. David and Nadine. They're well-known in the club. They've been together for over a year, but they don't have any safe words. They take their sessions to the extremes. It's intoxicating to watch, just as my Lilly is drawn to them, like a moth to a flame.

I stand next to Lilly for a moment, shifting my Barker Black shoes slightly across the cement floor. Her eyes dart toward them, and her head tilts slightly. A sharp breath is pulled through my clenched teeth at the thought of my flogger smacking along her back. She should be still. Her back is curved. She has so much to learn. I pivot and face her, but I don't address her; I'm merely letting her feel my presence.

From the way her breathing picks up, I know she's filled with anticipation as well. She's practically trembling beneath me.

I already know her name, since I've heard her tell it to a few others in the club. But I feel compelled to ask anyway, as if it's the polite thing to do. I crouch down next to her, my hand resting gently on her head. Her soft blonde hair is like silk beneath the rough pads of my fingers. The strands slide easily through my fingers and whether it's unconscious or not, Lilly leans slightly into my touch. Her eyes close, and her plump lips part. She is a woman in need of approval. And desperately in need of touch.

I clear my throat as I take my hand away, testing her obedience and knowledge. She remains in place, her eyes locked on the floor, although her tongue darts out quickly, wetting the seam of her lips. I wait a moment, rising to stand, but she still doesn't move. Good girl. It's not until I give her permission to look, that her pale blue eyes lift to reach mine. As soon as her baby blues meet my gaze with a look of pure desire, tiny golden flecks swirling in the mist of blue and sparkling with lust, I feel a spark between us that sets my heart afire.

This is the closest we've ever been; the first time I've ever touched her. I almost have to reach out to brace myself, surprised by the electricity flowing through me. It's the intensity in her eyes, the vulnerability that shocks me. I hadn't anticipated how emotional she would be so quickly, how trusting. Maybe it's in her nature. I don't like to think that way though. I want it to be just for me, and only me. The sight of her eyes in this moment will stay with me once we've parted, I know that.

"What name do you go by?" I ask her easily, ignoring the attraction screaming at me to claim her right here, right now.

"Lilly," she replies, and her voice is low and gentle. *Lilly*. It suits her. I call her by her name for the first time, letting the soft sounds of her name fall from my lips.

"And you?" she asks, chancing a look up at me, her doe eyes calling to me in a way where I almost feel a need to look in another direction. To break the intense contact, but I don't. I accept the challenge. "You can call me Sir," I tell her. She licks her bottom lip, her eyes darting away as her breath leaves her, and then quickly looks back to meet my gaze. I smirk down at her and ask, "Does that turn you on?"

I already know it does, but hearing the "yes" fall from her plump lips gives me undeniable satisfaction.

Nadine moans from across the room and then hisses in a sharp breath that echoes off the walls. It distracts us both. David has a lit candle above her, a match in his hand while keeping the fire on the wick. The wax slowly drips down onto her naked body, leaving splashes of red covering her milky white skin. She's bound to the bench on her back, unable to move very much, but each time the wax hits her she wiggles slightly to get away.

I faintly hear David admonishing her. "You need to be still, my love." Immediately, she stops writhing on the bench, her head falling back, and her mouth opening in a silent scream as the next drop of wax falls between her breasts. Her hands ball into fists and her feet move outward slightly, but the rest of her body remains perfectly still as she obeys her Master.

"Do you want to watch them?" I ask Lilly softly, gently lifting her chin and drawing her attention back to me.

She starts to look up at me. But she stops herself. "I would like to. If you would allow it." She barely whispers the second sentence. My dick hardens instantly, loving the vulnerability in her voice, loving the way she gives me power. And reveling in the fact that she's uncertain about her behavior. It's the uncertainty that makes me crave her as a Submissive. She's breakable. And I fucking love that about her.

"Are you playing with me, my flower?" I ask her in a deep rough voice.

Her eyes look up into mine, widening as my words register. She stutters to answer, her breath coming in quicker. Fear flashes in her eyes, not understanding what I'm asking her. I give her a soft smile to put her at ease and say softly, yet in a stern voice, "Meaning that you want me to play the role of your Master?"

I can practically see the relief flooding through her veins. The tension leaves her body as she looks up and answers me confidently, "I would like to play." The strength in her voice diminishes as she adds, "I'm not sure if I need a Dominant or a Master."

Submissives have more power than they realize. They truly control the relationship. They set the boundaries, they start and stop all acts with what they allow the Dominant to get away with. The Dominant has an illusion of control. I'm not interested in an illusion. I want absolute power. I want to be her Master.

"I'm not looking for a Submissive, my flower," I state clearly. I don't want her to get the wrong impression. I'll determine her boundaries, then I'll push her much faster than she's pushing herself.

Her eyes quickly look beyond me, staring at the row of cages that line the left wall as she considers what I'm saying. "I'm willing to play with you, for now." My body heats, and adrenaline pumps through my veins with an anxiety I'm uncomfortable with, something I've not yet experienced. I don't want her denying me.

She nods her head slowly.

"So would you like to play with me then?" I ask her.

"As a Slave?" she asks me, clarifying what I've just said.

I tower over her small body. "In this setting it doesn't matter. We'll only play for a moment."

Her forehead pinches slightly as she considers what I'm saying. "You'll do as I say while we're down here. And if you don't like it, you can simply leave."

She seems dumbstruck by my words at first, and the connection between us wanes as something else settles in between us. Insecurity. She's confused and uncertain not about what she should do, but about what I can give her.

I'm quick to put her at ease as I say, "You can always leave.

33

Regardless of whether I'm your Master or Dominant. You can always leave without fear." Her expression softens as she comprehends what I'm telling her. In a sense, I'm twisting words to put her at ease so I can keep her. But I don't give a damn. I'll do what I must to get what I want.

Her voice comes in breathy as she responds, "I think I'd like to play."

"Good girl." My lips curve into a noticeable smile, and when she responds with a faint huff of a breath, it's slow and easy. And sexual. Everything about her right now from her posture and dilated pupils, to the way she's breathing and clenching her thighs depicts how turned on she is by my approval.

I walk over to the bench while she remains kneeling. I'm highly aware of the other men in the room, but there's no way they'd approach her. They'd be dead men if they dared to try.

I want her in my lap while we watch, grinding on my hard cock. She gets up on all fours before I tell her to, eager to come over to me. I wonder if she wants to crawl, if she wants to be degraded. I've yet to learn her limits. I'm confident that *she* doesn't even know her limits. But I'm going to find them by pushing them.

I need to see what her true fantasy is, and how much she can take. It may frighten her, but she'll thank me in the end.

"Come to me." I give her the command and wait for her reaction. She immediately crawls to me. Watching her move catlike across the floor, her bare knees against the cold, hard ground and her nightie riding up high on the back of her thighs while she obeys my command so swiftly, turns me the fuck on. It makes me harder than I've ever been before. As soon as she gets to me, I reach down and lift her up by her hips, settling her in my lap. She lets out a gasp at my powerful grip, which only makes my cock throb harder for her.

That sound. I want to hear it again and again and again.

I grip her by the nape of her neck. A powerful hold, yet I'm still gentle, barely holding her still in my grasp. Her body is so much lighter than I had anticipated. It's easy to move her, to grip her hips and direct her body which way I want it to go. Feeling the weight of her ass in my lap I can only imagine how easily I can take her. Her petite, pear-shaped body was meant to take a punishing fuck.

"You came down here for a reason, my flower." My hot breath tickles her cheek, causing her to shiver slightly.

"Yes, Sir," she says staring straight ahead, but she turns to me, looking me in the eyes as she adds, "I'm curious."

The focus of the dungeon is pain. The name is fitting, and we're gathered down here because the things that happen in the confines of these walls may be disturbing to others. I've watched Nadine and David before. I enjoy their play. I've also seen much, much worse. But what they do is nothing short of erotic to me.

"Put your hands behind your back." Lilly looks at me hesitantly, but even as she does, she obeys me, putting both of her hands behind her back and balancing herself by shifting slightly in my lap. I want to get rid of that hesitation. The more she plays with me, the more she'll learn to trust.

My dick throbs against her soft ass, and I know she has to feel it. I shift in my seat, making sure it presses deep into her flesh, allowing her to feel the pulsating thickness. I want her to know how much I want her.

There are rope ties, leather belts and all sorts of instruments of bondage in a storage bench next to me. More different varieties hang on the wall on hooks to my right. I'm quick to choose a hobble for its versatility and ease of use.

It's a wide piece of leather with holes in it for a buckle, complete with D rings and O rings so that the band can be used as restraint, like handcuffs or, without the rings, a simple collar. I wrap the leather around her wrist and secure it and then do the same to the other wrist before fastening the two ends together with the buckle.

I make sure that both are tightened and fastened all the way so that her wrists are completely restrained behind her.

"I want a safe word," Lilly speaks quickly, her words laced with fear, as I tuck the leather strap into the loop. I can practically hear her heart beating faster and faster, mixing in with the sounds of Nadine's pleasure.

A scowl forms on my face and knots my forehead. I fucking hate safe words. I'll know her limits before she does. I'm good at reading people, and I know the difference between pleasure and pain all too well.

I can feel the eyes of the guards on me, no longer watching the scene unfold in the center of the room. Instead they're focused on the two of us, and my reaction to her wanting a safe word. My body heats with anger. But I need to get the fuck over it, she's only just now let me hold her. She's never done this before. She'll learn.

"And what would you like that word to be?" I ask her. I don't miss the look of surprise on some bastard's face across the room when I give in so easily. I don't know his name, and I don't give a fuck; he's seated across the room and enjoying the show. And not the one starring David and Nadine.

"Lollipop," Lilly answers quickly.

I almost huff out a laugh at her answer. *Lollipop?* Does she think this shit is funny? That it's some sort of a joke? I furrow my brow for a moment and then I nod my head, shoving the anger down. It doesn't matter if she thinks this is a game, she won't be thinking that once I'm done with her.

"Lollipop it is then." I lean forward, placing my lips

just barely against the shell of her ear and whisper, "Now that I've given it to you, you need to make sure that you use it wisely." Her thighs clench in my lap as she nods her head. I quickly spread her thighs apart, gripping both her knees in my hands and placing her legs outside of my own. The shocked gasp that spills from her lips at how quickly I've made her available to me makes my lips curve up.

My hand slips between her thighs, my fingers barely caressing her skin. I make sure that my movements are slow, not so that she can see them coming, but just so I can send a chill of goosebumps down her body as I slide my fingertips along her soft skin. I want her to *feel* everything. I want her soaking wet by the time I slide my fingers inside her tight cunt.

I run my finger down the center of her lace panties. And again I whisper, "Next time you'll take these off before you come here." A soft moan escapes her lips as I brush my fingernail against her clit, back and forth. "Do you understand?"

"Yes, Sir," she breathes her answer. Her nipples are hardened and poking through the thin fabric of her nightgown. I want to take it off and suck her nipples into my mouth, swirling my tongue around them and heightening her pleasure. But not here. Not with everyone watching. I need to take her home. But I have to be patient. She needs to learn, and I need to find her limits.

Fuck, she makes me so fucking hard. I want to take her right now, thrusting my dick into that wet, tight pussy of hers.

My back hits the concrete wall as I spread my knees wider, which in turn spreads hers. She bites down on her bottom lip, but she has no protests. I push the thin lace fabric away and run my fingers over her soaking wet lips and groan in the crook of her neck. "You're so ready for me." Her eyes close as a shiver runs down her body.

I'll focus on her clit as she watches the scene. She's so fucking responsive. I'm in awe of how beautiful the subtle changes of her pleasure are expressed on her face. "You are going to watch what a Master does to his Slave," I lean a little closer, gently kissing the lobe of her ear and then adding in a softer voice, "and you're going to get off to it, but only when I say."

She nods her head and immediately answers, "Yes, Sir."

I grip the nape of her neck, not hard, just enough that she knows I have control of her positioning. With her wrists bound, her legs spread, one of my hands between her thighs and the other on the nape of her neck, I have complete control over her.

A silver gleam shines across the room as David produces a knife. He scrapes the wax from Nadine's body, the knife tickling her skin as he does it.

Nadine whimpers as he gets close to her hardened nipple, scraping her sensitive skin but careful not to cut her. She moans as the sensation becomes overwhelming. Every little touch gives her pleasure. Even those that are dangerous.

"It's a good thing that she learned to be still," I whisper in Lilly's ear, careful not to disturb the scene. A few other members of the club have gathered and are watching. Scenes like this are rare in the club. It takes a lot to trust someone so wholeheartedly. Most have their eyes on the couple in the center of the room. These two always manage to draw a crowd.

But some of the men are focused on us.

I run my fingers down her lips all the way to her entrance, teasing her and then trace back up to her clit. I'm toying with her and testing her sensitivity. "She must have so much trust in him." I kiss her neck, breathing in her scent. So sweet. She's truly a flower.

I open my eyes and see that David has traveled down Nadine's body, flicking off the wax as he goes along with the knife. The skin on her belly is red from the pressure of the blade. The sensitive stroking of the sharp edge against her skin brings the endorphins to the surface. That's the entire point. It makes every feeling that much more intense. I watch as he travels down farther, crouching between her legs. A few drops of red wax have pooled and hardened around her pubic hair. And he scrapes them off, cutting the short hair as he goes.

I slip my middle finger down the center of Lilly's hot pussy, and then back up to her hard, throbbing clit, putting more and more pressure on her as I rub in hard circles. I pinch the hardened nub slightly as David leans in between Nadine's legs and begins licking her pussy.

I wasn't anticipating her to react so strongly, so quickly, but Lilly's body trembles and her thighs tense, immediately trying to close in my lap. Her head falls back, hitting my left shoulder and she moans loudly as she cums in my lap. My dick pulses with need at the knowledge that I brought her to her edge so quickly.

I make my strokes harder, rougher, making sure to get every bit of her orgasm out of her trembling body. She shakes in my grasp, my left hand moving from the nape of her neck to wrap around her waist, steadying her as her orgasm reverberates through her.

I stare at her in wonder, amazed by how fucking beautiful she is. It only makes me want to get her off even more.

Her body wavers in my grasp, completely unsteady, unhinged from the intensity of her orgasm. I've seen her touching herself before, but it was nothing like this. I should admonish her for cumming without permission. A wicked grin slips into place on my lips. My sweet girl needs to be punished. She's really going to enjoy this.

Before I can move her back to my chest and spread her wider so I can feel the arousal dripping down her pussy and onto my lap, she calls out to me, "Lollipop."

Her eyes are wide open, seemingly just as shocked as I am. I hesitate, but only for a moment. Only because I'm pissed. I don't want a safe word; I know she doesn't need it. I feel ripped off in some ways. My grip on her tightens for a moment, hating whatever I've done to make her safe word me. I imagine it was the intensity of the situation. I can only begin to guess that's why. Unless she knew her punishment was looming...

I'm quick to unbind the hobble around her wrists. Not because I want to, and certainly not because she can't handle this. Only because I agreed to it.

"I'm sorry," she breathes the apology, her breath coming in faster. "I just didn't-"

She doesn't finish, looking up at me with wide eyes shining with fear and shock. I press my finger to her lips. "This is new to you. You're going to be surprised by what I can do to your body, by what arouses you. Don't let it scare you."

She swallows thickly and starts to apologize again, but I won't allow it. She seems genuinely upset. But I don't want her to remember this moment with a single negative thought.

Still hard and pissed that I wasn't able to bind her to the Saint Andrew's Cross and give her a lashing, I steady her on her feet and stand behind her. "Don't apologize, my flower. You did very well." She could have done better. If only she'd given me more control. But that requires trust. And I'm willing to wait to earn it.

As I lead her out of the dungeon, I pass a few men. All of

them wear masks, but their eyes follow us as I walk by them, a look flashing in their eyes that lets me know what they think of me. None of them trust me. But I don't give a fuck. I don't trust them either.

Even here in this dungeon beneath a house of sin, I can't escape my past.

CHAPTER 5

Lilly

A RUSH of endorphins flows through my limbs, filling me with excitement as the previous day's events run through my mind. I'm trying to remember everything as I prepare to write, sitting at my Ikea desk in the corner of my living room.

I've never felt anything like this before. I've never had someone own me so utterly and completely. So quickly taking possession of me. The feel of that masked man's hard body pressed up against mine, the way he took control of me, his hard cock pressing against me, throbbing and pulsating, making me want to beg for it…

I have no idea what came over me, submitting to him like that. But I don't regret one moment of the experience. It was so intoxicating that even now my body refuses to relax, little jolts of electricity shocking my nerves throughout the morning. I can already see myself mirroring a scene in my book, making it even hotter and heavier than what went down in that dungeon room. What I wish had taken place afterward if my fear hadn't made me safe word.

Fuck. I'm already getting wet, and the day hasn't even started yet.

Shaking my head to clear it, I open up my laptop and bring up the desktop. I need to write to get my mind off my sinful thoughts. Before I can open my Word document and begin writing the scene that won't leave me alone, I see an email notification pop up on my screen followed by the tell-tale *ding*.

From: Zach White
   To: Ms. Lilly Wade
   Subject: I need ur help.

Hey, I know ur probably busy with ur family over vacation and all, and I really hate to bother u, but can u do me a favor? I got myself into some major shit and now I have to do community service if I don't want to end up in juvey. I'm not going into details about what happened because I don't want u to be pissed off at me. I remember the talk we had before the semester ended and I'm really ashamed that I didn't listen.

I'm lucky as fuck tho. The judge said he might let me choose where I put in my hours if I show him that I'm really sorry, but it has to be something that he will approve of. Right now, they have me signed up for public bathroom cleaning. I can't do it. Public bathrooms make my skin crawl. Like seriously, I'm a total germaphobe after the shit mom put me thru with her dirty fucking needles and pipes all over the place and those cockroaches she had crawling everywhere. I know it's shitty to ask, but can you please help? Could you get me assigned somewhere else or something?

I can fucking hardly stand it when I have to use one at school and there is no goddamn way I'm doing that shit unless I have to.

Zach

I sit back in my chair as I read his words. My first reaction is to respond and tell him to just grow up and deal with it. Cleaning a public bathroom, while pretty gross, is a small price to pay in exchange for not winding up in a more serious place. I'm pissed off, too. We had so many talks, and I poured my heart and soul into every single one of them, about him getting his act together and putting more effort into his schooling. And figuring out where he wanted to be in a few years. He could do great things. We set up a plan together, and he promised that he'd do better.

But then I remember all the things he's gone through, and my anger subsides.

Zach was dealt some rough cards coming into this world. He had an abusive father who beat him regularly before he abandoned him, leaving him with a mother who was strung out on drugs and let her son live in absolute squalor, resulting in his germaphobia. He's just a kid in so many ways. I could see the pain in his eyes every day that he came into my office, the hurt that haunted him. Seeing that tore at my heart. No child should have to go through what he went through. I let out a soft sigh as I position my fingers over the keyboard. I can't be angry with him, that's not going to help him. Without someone in his life that shows that they care about him, he might as well give up. I can't let that happen.

No matter what bad thing he's done, I have to offer what help I'm able. I refuse to give up on him, and I refuse to let him give up on himself.

But I can't enable him either.

Blowing my bangs out of my eyes, my fingers fly across the keys as I type my response.

From: Ms. Wade
    To: Zach White

Zach,

I'm so very sorry to hear that you've gotten yourself into some trouble, but I did warn you that if you kept on your current path, that something like this might happen. I'm not going to lie and say I'm not disappointed. I'm pissed, actually. I put a lot of time and effort into trying to help you, and it doesn't look like it stuck with you. I hope that you're able to prove me wrong. I understand why you don't want to have to clean public bathrooms, given your past with your mother.

And I will try my best to figure out the options that are available to you… but only if you tell me what you did, and why. I want to help you, but I'm not going to let you walk all over me. I can't help you if I don't know what exactly you've been caught doing. I'm available to talk and work on the plan we've set for you. This is yet another obstacle that I know you'll overcome. I look forward to hearing from you.

Sincerely,
    Ms. Wade

I sigh again as I press send. My heart hurts, hating the fact

I can't give him an easy out. I can't just pluck him from where he is now and move him somewhere better, where he's surrounded by encouragement and more opportunities. This very situation is going to close even more doors for him, and I hate that simple truth. He's just made things harder on himself.

I hate that the kid is in this predicament and I feel really bad for being tough with him, but I can't let him off easy. He can't come asking for my help and then try to gloss over the crime he committed. I hope he does the right thing and comes clean. I really like him and want to see him do something with his life, not end up a deadbeat father, or a druggie like his mom, living a life of crime.

Helping troubled students like Zach gives my life meaning, and it means a lot to me. There are times where I wish I could just wave my hand and change all of their lives for the better. Ha, if only such magic existed. The world would be a much better place. But sometimes... I just have to admit...

You can't help them all. They need to want to change. And I don't know if Zach really does or not.

Ugh. Just thinking about how helpless I feel in the moment, makes me depressed. I need to try to write, get my mind off this.

After making a mental note to check my email for his response later, I go back to my Word document. For the next five minutes I sit there looking at the blinking cursor trying to think of what to write. Nothing comes to me. It's frustrating. I have so much material from the previous day, yet I can't write a single word. Seriously, my fingers should be flying across the keys like a roadrunner, filling the screen with steamy paragraphs that would have even the most chaste woman wanting to go on a date with Mr. Rabbit.

I let out a frustrated sigh.

I guess I'm just not in the mood to write anymore.

Sighing again, I get up from my desk and go over to my bookshelves and begin rummaging through my erotic romance sections. There's nothing like a good book to pull me out of a slump. I grab one with a shirtless hot guy with six pack abs on the cover, entitled *Deep Inside*. I already know what I'm getting with such a title, and I'm hoping it's just what I need to forget about my depressing work. Some days are hard. But it makes the good days that much better.

I settle down in my favorite recliner and begin reading. After a couple of paragraphs, I decide that I need something hotter. I skip straight to the first sex scene, but after several paragraphs of that, I find my mind wandering. The words are filled with passion, but I don't feel any of it. They seem dry. Empty. It doesn't even begin to compare to...

My mind wanders back to my masked Sir that I submitted to the day before, and the sadness I feel falls away. Images of how he handled my body and how he got me off flash before my eyes. A soft moan escapes my lips.

God, it was so hot, so incredibly intense. Just thinking about it now, leaves me breathless. The intensity of my orgasm and how he controlled me made me call out the safe word without even realizing it.

Lollipop.

I huff out a little giggle at the word. I don't know what I was thinking when I told him that I wanted it to be that. Maybe I thought it was cute. He didn't look like he thought it was, but in the end, he didn't care. He was more concerned with my body and pushing me to my limits.

I think I pissed him off by saying it. But I couldn't help myself. I was overwhelmed.

One thing that keeps bothering me though, is that he didn't show any commitment to me. He didn't ask for my number, or show any interest in following me from the club. He let me leave without mentioning anything, other than not wearing underwear next time. It's not like that's a normal occurrence. I'm sure there are rules against men following a woman from the club, but it still would have made me feel special if he'd asked me for more. I sure as fuck want more.

I'm curious to see where this goes. I've read all about BDSM, and I've researched Master and Slave relationships. I figure that I can at least try this if he pursues me, knowing the only way I'll really understand a M/s relationship is if I experience it for myself. My knowledge from reading about it makes me feel confident that I can handle it. It's a win-win relationship for me. I get to explore this dark sexual world, and further my research for my book at the same time.

Still, the forbidden and dark aspects keep me from committing fully. Thank fuck for Club X. A knock on the door pulls me out of my reverie. Clearing my throat, I get up to see what it is. The postal truck is driving off when I open the door, and down at my feet there's a large parcel sitting on my front steps, a beautiful white box with a white bow tied around it. Furrowing my brow with curiosity, I pick it up. It's rather light for its size, and I take it inside, setting it down on the kitchen table.

As I unwrap the item from the tissue paper, I can't stop the gasp that escapes from my lips, my heart skipping a beat. It's a rather revealing white lace dress that is see-through in seductive places. My cheeks flame with a blush at the thought of wearing it. As I hold it up to the light, my heart races.

It's so beautiful. Luxurious and obviously expensive. And exactly my size. As I press it up against my chest, the significance isn't lost on me. Tonight, Club X's theme is all white. I can hardly wait. I set the dress on the table, but something brushes against my arm. I look down.

There's a note attached to the dress. I pick it up, and my heart only speeds up even faster as I read the simple words.

I'll see you tonight, my flower.
    Your Sir.

CHAPTER 6

Joseph

As I wait at the long mahogany bar at the front entrance of Club X just outside of the foyer, I take another look at the text from my brother. I don't know why I do this to myself. I have no intention of texting him back. There's no reason for me to be involved at all with my family anymore. They have nothing to offer me, and I have nothing to offer them, despite what my brother seems to think.

Roberto may be a few years younger, but he'll be the one taking over the *familia*. I don't need to listen to a damn thing that he says right now though. I sure as fuck don't have to listen to my father either.

I'm not getting sucked back into that life. I have no intention of going back to them. I'm not going to be a puppet for them. I'm not going to take over like I was supposed to. I played my part and took the fall; I'm done with them.

I don't ever expect to live a normal life. I know that's not meant for a man like me.

I wasn't brought up to be normal. There are things I've

done that are unforgivable. The sins of my past will always stay with me, and they made me into the man I am. Whether I like that or not, it's true. My own mother was a whore. My father, Angelo, and the Don of the Levi *familia*, wanted sons, so he knocked several women up, one after the other, until he was given two boys. I grew up surrounded by prostitutes and drug cartels. I've sat through dinners that were ended with gunshots or stabbings. It was normal, and there was never a moment where safety was a possibility. There was a promise of loyalty, but in actuality any and everyone was waiting to stab one another in the back.

That's the kind of life I'd be living. It's the shit that I lived through. Even when I left the *familia*, my past followed me. My name still follows me.

Not responding to my brother, half-brother really, sends a strong message. I don't give a fuck though. I have no intention of sending one back. There's no reason for us to meet up. We have nothing in common. I have a conscience. It may have taken me a long time to find a way out, but I have a desire to lead a different life, even if I'm already condemned to hell. My brother doesn't share that desire. All he cares about is money, greed and selfishness. I wouldn't be surprised if he kills our father one day. Not that I'll shed any tears over it. They're both despicable for what they've done.

I have enough money I never need to work a day in my life again, one of the unforeseen bonuses of having the Romanos' funds sent to my account. It was meant to be evidence used against me, but never came to fruition. I need a new life; I need something to look forward to. Something to give me purpose.

I think back to Lilly, and my hand gently starts swirling the whiskey in the tumbler. She more than interests me. I click the button on the side of the phone before slipping it back into my pocket and take a swig. The burn does nothing to soothe the sickness stirring in the pit of my stomach at the thought of Lilly not coming back.

I know I need to be gentle with her. I can't be the ruthless man that I used to be. I need to hide the darkness that's inside me as best as I can until I have her fully and completely trusting me. I need to get the fuck out of here, too.

The couples walk around me, the Submissives completely unknowing, nor do they care who I am. Most of their eyes are focused on the ground. Some of the men walk by me without taking a second look, but most of them hold contempt for me. The newspapers crucified me, as they should have. My name is practically a slur. I look up at the one man that dares to give me a hard look. The moment my eyes meet his, he breaks his gaze, pretending to stare past me. Fucking coward.

I look to my right, signaling the bartender for one more. There's a two-drink limit in Club X for obvious reasons, but my tolerance is high enough now that the drinks hardly have an effect on me. As the bartender catches my eye, I notice a man to my right staring at me once again.

It's Zander. Zander Payne. I'm well aware of who he is and what he's capable of. Even if most of the men in here have no idea. I snort at the thought. He's someone the men here should truly be afraid of.

There's an odd look on Zander's face. A look like he has something to say.

I hold his gaze as the bartender sets my glass of whiskey down on the counter in front of me. I wrap my fingers around the glass and bring it to my lips, not moving my eyes off Zander. He doesn't drop his gaze either.

I've never said a single word to the man. I've never said a word to any of the men here except for Isaac, the head of security, but that was brief and inconsequential. I have no fucking reason to talk to them.

I only came as a favor to Kiersten. She was worried about me. She's always worried about everything and everyone.

As the whiskey burns down my throat and fills my chest with the heat I've come to rely on for comfort, Zander finally walks toward me with purposeful steps. He has to walk around a few of the couples. One girl notices Zander walking by and obviously pushes her breasts up and out. She's sitting on a stool leaning forward, her white lingerie wrapped around her body and tied around her neck. Her head lowers until she looks up at him through her thick lashes, attempting to be submissive, although she's doing a poor job of it. But he ignores her.

Just as he ignores all the women here. No one else may see it, but I know the only reason Zander's here is for business. He likes to keep an eye on his assets. He likes to have an eye over everyone around him. That's just the man he is. And I truly admire it, although it's hard to admit that. I do the opposite, I try to stay away from anything and everything that reminds me of what I used to be. The only problem is I have no idea what that leaves me with.

"Mr. J? Is that what you go by here?" Zander asks me, standing a few feet from me as he rests his hand against the bar, in a seemingly casual stance.

"I prefer Sir." I set the whiskey down and leave it there, squaring my shoulders and waiting for him to say whatever it is that's on his mind.

"Ah," he says easily. This is the way he approaches all things in his life. With a casual air that makes him seem harmless. Charming, even. But I know what he's capable of. I've seen it firsthand. Everyone owes him but me. And I won't be making any business deals with a cunning shark like him.

"Sir?" He lets out a small laugh while shoving his hands into his pockets and looking past me. "I was wondering when you were going to begin indulging."

I don't respond to him. I'm not sure if he's referring to Lilly, or my bid on the auction last month. Either way, I don't give a fuck. What I do in here and outside of the club is none of his business. The less this man knows about me, the better. I look past him, toward the front entrance, waiting for Lilly. I know that she received my package. I'm only curious whether or not she's decided to obey me, to wear the dress I've given her and to come without any undergarments on. The latter is what I'm truly curious about. Not only did I give her the order yesterday, but from what I know about her, it's out of her element to be so brazen.

Zander shrugs as he says, "Not that it's any of my concern." He signals the bartender and orders a draft beer.

"Is there something you wanted to ask me, Zander?" I say to get to the point and end this charade.

His pretty boy face flashes a smirk, although he still staring at the back wall where the shelves of liquor bottles are lined up. "I may have heard something I thought you would be interested in knowing."

A man walks quickly in our direction. I've seen him before a time or two, although his name doesn't come to memory. He's a businessman, not someone that I would ever be involved with in the past. Although he does seem to know who I am, judging by the way he avoids my gaze at all cost. The last time I saw him was while I was in the dungeon with Lilly. I search around him for his pet, Adela, but she's absent today. My blood simmers, thinking he's hurt her again. Kiersten told me about him, about an *incident*. I glare at the man, hating that I have to share the same air he breathes. He clears his throat as he pats Zander's right shoulder, taking his attention away from me.

"Master Z," he says, and the man's voice is rougher and lower than I would've anticipated. My eyes hone in on a bruise at his throat, like fingers still wrapped around his windpipe. I look back at Zander and put two and two together. I back away slightly, turning and giving them privacy. Before I can turn from them completely, I notice Zander's annoyance with the man. He looks at the man's hand pointedly before responding in a low voice laced with a threat, "Yes?"

The man seems fidgety, leaning forward and whispering not so softly, "If you have a minute, I'd like to talk."

Zander nods at the man and then turns back to me, grabbing the beer off the bar.

"If you want to talk," Zander says to me, only looking me in the eyes for a moment as he stands. The permanent smile on his face is nowhere to be seen, "I heard something you may be interested in knowing." Without anything else he leaves, walking from the bar of Club X down the hallway with the man following him and away from the onlookers.

I have no idea what he could have heard, or why it would concern me. I'm not willing to make a deal with him, but I won't deny that I'm the least bit curious. My eyes follow the two men as they disappear from view.

I down what's left in my glass, setting it on the bar behind me as I swallow the amber liquid.

As soon as the glass tumbler hits the wooden bar, the doors open for Lilly. The bouncer gives her a small nod and she continues forward with confidence, both hands gripping her wristlet. She's in a long trench coat that goes down to her knees, although her calves are bare. Her high heels are nude with rose gold tips and matching rose gold heels.

She walks to the desk to check her coat, just as most of the other guests do. Some walk past her and make their way past me and off to the right down the hall to the private rooms. Many guests here don't even bother with the public. They just like the privacy and protection that the club offers. The black and white tweed trench coat slips off her shoulders down to her elbows, exposing her bare back from the white lace halter dress that I've given her.

She's a vision dressed all in white. The shimmering silk only makes her tanned skin look that much more kissable. As she takes off the coat, it brushes against the hem of the dress, pulling it up slightly and unbeknownst to her, showing more of her upper thigh. Several men around her take in the sight of her gorgeous curves. She doesn't notice them. She doesn't realize how tempting she is. I could wait for her to come to me. She's obedient. And the fact that she wore the dress I sent her, signifies that she wants me still.

After seeing the two of us interact in the dungeon, she'll be getting more attention than she ever did before. So long as I don't put a collar around her neck.

But I'm not going to give any of these men a chance to come between us.

I push off of the bar, walking straight toward her as she hands her coat to the man behind the counter.

I'm going to make sure they all stay away and that they know she's mine.

CHAPTER 7

Lilly

I STEP INTO CLUB X, my limbs trembling with excitement, my eyes taking in the themed decorations. There's white everywhere, the usual red sconces on the wall giving off a soft, pure glow, the tables decorated with silk ivory table-cloths, and even the walls have been draped with temporary white lace curtains, giving the ballroom an almost heavenly feel.

The air inside the club seems to crackle, only adding to the anxiety twisting in my stomach. Keeping in with the theme, everyone is dressed in white finery. I inhale in a sharp breath as my eyes flit about the room, in awe of the other women. They all look gorgeous, angelic even. The men still wear masks, but they're all white.

If I didn't know any better, I would think the attendees were dressed to gain entry to the gates of heaven, or a slutty version anyway, I imagine. I huff out a small laugh at the thought. It's comical when I think about it. I'm pretty sure with all the debauchery and fornication that goes on under this roof, everyone here is going straight to hell. Worry mingles in with my excitement as I peer down at my white lace dress that Sir gifted me. I think I look alright in comparison to the other Submissives and Slaves, but it's hard not to feel a sense of inadequacy. I thought I looked good in it back at home, but I'm slightly nervous that I may disappoint him. *My Sir.*

Slowly, I remove the overcoat from around my shoulders, the cool air of the club hitting my flesh and causing goosebumps to travel over every inch of my body. I shiver at the sensation, my nipples almost pebbling against the soft white fabric as it shifts against my skin. That's when I see *him* over at the bar, his intense, dark eyes boring into mine. My heart skips a beat as I gaze back into his handsome visage. He looks heavenly, dressed in an all-white suit, and I love how his white winged mask frames his chiseled features. His hard jawline and piercing eyes remind me somewhat of Thor, but I know this hero would rather wield a whip than a hammer.

My breathing quickens as I stare at him, my mind filled with the image of him wielding a whip. My skin pricks from the desire that flows up from my stomach.

His eyes seem to call to me with hypnotic power, and before I know it, I'm moving toward him without even thinking about it. My coat falls into the hands of the coat check attendee, quickly forgotten. By the time he reaches me, I feel as though I'm completely under his control. He could tell me to jump, and I wouldn't even ask how high. I'd just do it.

Up close, he's even more handsome than he was from across the room, putting my memory of him to shame. His white suit is crisp and spotless, his winged mask glinting in the soft lighting. His eyes, which are a deep brown, continue to hold my gaze, enchanting me with their intensity. My legs tremble, and it's hard not to show the anxiety coursing through my limbs as I resist the urge to reach out and run my fingertips along his chiseled jawline, wanting to feel him to make sure he's real.

I can't believe this is the same man that took control of my body the other night. The man who wanted me. The man I safe worded and walked away from.

I swallow as I take in all of him in his majestic glory, barely remembering to breathe. He's almost too sexy to be real. He radiates a kind of cold power that makes me shiver, his eyes filled with dark secrets I know should horrify me, but only serve to turn me on even more. It's an odd contrast, the darkness in his eyes, and the pure white he's wearing, but I fucking love it.

For a moment, I consider kneeling before him. I've seen other women do it, but I'm not sure if I should. I'm not even sure what we are, or what this is yet. He's not my Master, and yet...

He chuckles as he appraises me, his deep rich baritone sending electric shocks through my clit. "Do you like it?" he asks, his dark eyes sparkling with amusement. He must be able to sense my anxiety and uncertainty, and it pleases him immensely. "Like what?" I ask breathlessly, trying in vain to seem confident.

He smiles at me broadly. "Your dress."

I know he thinks I must be a fucking idiot. How could I be so clueless? What else could he have been talking about? The snow in Antarctica?

It's because he's so damn hot that I can't think around him, I tell myself. I blush furiously, my cheeks flaming. "I do, thank you," I reply.

"You mean 'thank you, Sir'," he corrects me firmly, an eyebrow arched sternly.

My skin pricks at my mistake, the heat of shame making it feel as if my cheeks might burn off. "Sorry, Sir. I thank you so much for the dress, Sir. It's beautiful." My words almost trip over themselves to get out. My heart seems to trip in my chest as well.

His eyes roll over my curves, and my skin tingles everywhere they seem to go. "Beautiful," he agrees huskily. I can only stand his hungry gaze for a moment before I'm forced to look away. All I can hear is the thumping of my heart in my chest. He isn't having it. He cups my chin, forcing me to look back at him, and pulls me in close, his hot touch burning my flesh. As he gazes into my eyes I can almost feel the possessiveness radiating from him. It should make me want to run away, but it only draws me to him like a moth to a flame. I didn't think it possible, but I desire him even more than the night before.

"Come, my flower." His words are not a request, but an order. I *must* obey. *Flower*.

He leads me through the club, walking with a confidence that's undeniable. As we walk through the hall, several men look our way, but each time they do, my Sir looks at them as if daring them to challenge him, and they look away. I thrill at the power he radiates, impressed by how some of these men, who are powerful in their own right, don't want to fuck with him.

It makes me feel secure. *Safe*.

Still, I feel eyes on me as we walk past the playrooms. This is different now. Before I was hidden in plain sight, but now that I'm with *him*, they're all watching. I pick at the hem on the dress, realizing how self-conscious I feel as we walk down the darkened hallway, past the double bodyguards, and to the stairwell of the dungeon.

There are a few more people here than the night before. I wish it were empty; I want privacy, but that's not going to happen. All eyes turn on us as we enter the room. Even the couple who obviously had the attention of the crowd before, stops to stare at us. Anxiety twists my stomach, and I look away.

"Look at me," my Sir commands.

I bring my gaze up to his eyes, trying not to shiver. In the background, the couples go back to their sessions and I hear the sing of whips flying through the air and smacking against flesh, followed by pained, but pleasured cries.

"What are you most interested in?" he asks, his deep voice punctuated by another *smack*. I want to look at the couple, the woman writhing in her rope binds as the man alternates the vibrator and the whip.

I shake my head, trying to keep my gaze focused on him as another lusty cry echoes off the walls. "I'm not sure. There's so much…" my voice trails off as I try to find the words. My heart won't stop racing in this room, especially standing here with him. I don't want to tell him that I'm partly here for research, and that I want to live out the fantasies I've read about in my favorite erotic romance novels. He might not like that. It'll only give him more evidence of my inexperience.

His eyes search my face. "Why do you keep coming down here?" he asks.

Smack. Smack. Smack. Another cry assaults my ears. "The pain," I whisper almost as if in response to the cracking of the whip and the cries that follow. "I'm curious." I swallow thickly and add, "I want to know why they beg for more."

He arches an inquisitive brow, the trace of a smile on his lips. The thought that I've pleased him with that knowledge makes my pussy heat for him. "Have you been whipped before?"

I shake my head vigorously, my breath quickening, my nipples pebbling. "No."

A grin plays across his firm lips as if my reply delights him in a way that I can't imagine. "Would you like to?" he asks, his deep voice dipping lower than I thought possible.

My heart races as I gaze into his eager expression, my pussy clenching with need. "Yes," I whisper. I've read about the pleasure it can bring. Every scene I've read turned me on with a passion that surprised me, and now I get to experience this sensation firsthand. I'm excited to see what it's like, but also apprehensive. To be completely honest, I'm terrified.

"Come." Taking my hand, he leads me over to the Saint Andrew's Cross. I watch as he loosens the leather straps on the cross, my legs slightly trembling, my pulse racing. His grip on my wrist is firm as he binds it to the cross. And then the other.

A guard I hadn't noticed before steps forward, a serious expression on his face.

"Lollipop is her safe word," Sir says before the guard can say anything, his voice laced with irritation. He doesn't even turn to face the guard as he straps my ankles to the cross, spreading my legs. The cool air flows up my white dress, and my heart stalls as the guard looks at me, searching my face for any objection. I clear my throat and nod, trying to swallow my heart as it tries to climb out of my throat, then he steps back into the shadows. Sir moves on to binding my other ankle, as if nothing had happened. As he tightens the leather strap, a realization washes over me.

This is *real*.

My heart skips a beat and I swallow thickly. This is not a fantasy I've read about in my books. If he whips me, I'm really going to feel it. I gulp again, my chest rising and falling sporadically. Based on everything I've read; I should like it. Love it, even. At least... I hope.

But it's a fucking whip.

Trembling with anxiety, I watch as Sir grabs a cat o' nine

tails off the wall, and the ends of the braided tails look frayed. He holds it up for me to see before letting the tails tickle down my body, over the pure white silk and down my belly. To my surprise, they're soft to the touch, but at the same time thick and unforgiving.

My throat constricts as anxiety threatens to overwhelm me, and I find myself struggling a little against my binds as sweat beads my brow. I need to chill. I can endure this. I've read about it in my books. The pain mixes in with pleasure, and you don't feel it after a while. Or so they say.

I need to just keep telling myself that, and I'll be fine.

He runs the whip along my flesh again, and I almost laugh at the sensation. It tickles. But I know it won't for long. I suck in a breath at the pain I know is coming.

Sir gentles his hand on my waist, his touch soft and comforting. "Relax, don't tense your body." His command is soft at the shell of my ear. His low voice is seductive and washes a sense of ease over me. My breathing still comes in deep, but this time it relaxes me. He relaxes me. I loosen my hands and try to ease my muscles. *Relax.* I must obey him. *Don't tense.*

"I could use this to make you feel… so many different things," Sir says, his breathing heavy and husky, and his eyes are darker than I've ever seen them. I know he's turned on by what he's about to do, but that still doesn't make me feel at ease.

Without another word, Sir pulls back his arm and then brings it forward with an almost animalistic grunt, the whip singing through the air.

Smack!

I gasp as the air is ripped from my lungs and the thick leather lashes my flesh, my raw cry ripping through the chamber. Fuck! It hurts, the sting bringing tears to my eyes. But at the same time, my nipples harden and my pussy clenches repeatedly around nothing, my breath coming in short, panting gasps as I try to recover.

I pull at the binds as Sir runs his fingers gently over the slight marks. From the pain, I expect the marks to be a bright red, maybe even breaking my skin, but they're merely a soft pink. All on my upper thighs. The throbbing pain dims instantly.

His touch is so soft, but it feels like electricity, directly connected to my clit. That's the best way I can explain it.

It's an odd sensation, feeling pain and pleasure at the same time, but I like it. The adrenaline that's rushing through my body is downright intoxicating.

Sir gazes at me, watching my reaction intently, his eyes blazing with intensity. "Did you like that, my flower?" His deep voice is low and husky, his breathing ragged. I can tell he enjoyed the lash as much as I did, his crotch sporting a huge bulge pressing against his dark pants. My mouth waters just looking at it.

"Yes," I whisper weakly, my limbs trembling uncontrollably, my palms moist and clammy as I clench my fists and teeth at the residual stinging pain.

He cocks a brow at me as he says, "Yes?"

I realize my mistake, but it's too late.

"Sir, my flower," he says as he twirls the whip a bit, watching the tails sing in the air. "You keep forgetting."

"I'm sorry, Sir."

I close my eyes, tensing my body.

"You should be punished," he says in a husky voice while he grips the tails of the whip in his left hand. "A little more pain this time."

The sing of the whip whistles in my ears followed by a powerful lash against my thighs that forces another raw cry from my lips.

The pain is more intense this time, making my skin prick

all over my body, my flesh red and heated in the areas where the leather tails have struck me. It's crazy what it does to me. It hurts like fuck, but it feels so good. I'm wrapped in almost dizzying euphoria, the room feeling as if it's spinning around me.

After a moment, I force my eyes open to see Sir gazing at me, an amused grin curling the corner of his lips.

"You will call me Sir," he says firmly with authority, his chest heaving from exertion. He put a lot of strength behind that last blow, and I can feel it, my flesh feeling like it's caught fire. The flames sending a hot sensation to my pussy.

"Yes, Sir," I gasp, barely able to fill my lungs with breath, my body teeming with pain and arousal.

The words haven't even finished leaving my lips before his fingers are tracing the marks and then his lips, and then his tongue. I hardly pay attention to it. Pain and pleasure become my existence as the room whirls around me, and my vision blurs almost to the point of darkness.

He pulls away from me while my eyes are closed. I instantly miss his soothing touch over the stinging heated marks.

Pain and pleasure, wrapped in leather. The sensation is addicting.

I want him to whip me again, harder, taking me to the next level, but a part of me knows I won't be able to take it. If he does it again, it will push me beyond the brink. I don't want to say it, but the word *lollipop* starts to form on my lips as I sense him preparing for another blow.

As if sensing what I'm about to say, Sir suddenly drops the whip to the floor, the loud clack on the floor making it obvious even with my eyes closed. He steps right in front of me, his shoes thudding against the stone floor, his breathing heavy and ragged from his exertion. Close up, I can see the sweat on his brow and the slight perspiration making his dress shirt cling to his chest. The smell of his masculinity fills my lungs and I breathe it in deeply, almost as if I'm inhaling a powerful drug.

"You've had enough, flower?" he asks me although we both know it's a statement, his deep, sexy voice low and filled with lust.

I'm unable to speak, my skin burning like it's on fire, but I manage to shake my head no. I can't be left like this. After that, I need a release. *Now.*

He grins at me, as if expecting my inability to answer, and runs his powerful fingers along my heated flesh, my skin stinging wherever he touches. A sibilant hiss of pain escapes my lips as I tremble with need at his touch, watching him trail his fingers down further until he reaches where I'm soaking wet.

He pulls his fingers away, and I instantly pull against the leather straps to bring his touch back to me. "Yes, Sir," I answer with the last bit of breath I have.

I watch him close his eyes, a satisfied groan leaving his lips at being able to touch my pussy as he feels my wet, dripping folds. I shiver at his seductive touch, moaning with pleasure.

"You're soaking wet for me, flower," he growls, slowly rubbing my clit in a circular motion, causing me to throw my head back and my eyelids to flutter. Fuck, his touch feels so good, heightened by the pain he's given me. I've read about this, but nothing could prepare me for it.

I want more of this, more of *him*. But before I can say anything, he suddenly curves his fingers into my pussy, stroking me hard and fast against my front wall. I cry out, fighting against my binds, my eyes rolling into the back of my head. I quickly forget the harsh pain stinging my skin, it feels so fucking good. Wet noises mix in with the pleasured cries of the other Submissives surrounding me as my thighs tremble around his arm, his fingers massaging the walls of my pussy. I let out several cries as I struggle against my binds, wanting to arch my back, but unable to. The intensity of the sensation is driving me wild, and I know I'm not going to be able to take it for much longer.

A thought makes my breath come to a halt, interrupting my pleasure for just a moment, although I'm not sure if he can tell. I've yet to be touched by a man. Not in any way. My anxiety courses through me, but the pleasure is too much.

Sir stares up at me as he pushes his fingers deeper inside of me, his eyes burning into my face, almost bidding me to cum for him. But all I can think is, *can he tell? Does he know my secret?* My head thrashes, and I close my eyes. I don't want to think about it. Right now, I'm someone else. It's only a fantasy.

I writhe against my binds, whipping my head this way and that way, crying out for release, a fiery crescendo building inside the pit of my stomach. *Fuck.* I can't take it. I'm about to cum.

Just as I'm about to find my release, Sir stops, leaving me gasping for breath, my forehead covered in a cold sweat. Anger surges through my breasts as I stare down at him in disbelief, my pussy clenching in fury as the orgasm it was chasing flees.

Sir rises to his feet and leans in, giving me an intensely hungry look as I breathe raggedly in his face. "You've been a good girl and you can cum, but I want to fuck you and make you cum on my dick," he explains as my lips part in protest.

His words should fill me with overwhelming excitement, but they don't.

My desire ebbs somewhat as I stare into his hungry eyes, a feeling of wariness washing over my limbs. I wasn't expecting it to go this far. Him getting me off with his fingers was fine, but I'm a virgin. And though he's sexy as sin, and turns me on like nothing I've ever felt before, I'm not going to give myself to him. Not like this. I don't even know his name.

A part of me wants it badly, though. As my breath comes in frantic pants, I can already imagine him plunging deep inside me with his thick cock, fucking me with a ferocity that would have me screaming with pleasure within seconds.

But I know it'll be a mistake.

Looking at the absolute hunger in his eyes, I feel the heavy weight of fear pressing down upon my chest, constricting my breathing.

I have to break this off before I cave to the desire he makes so hard to resist.

Lollipop, a voice urges in my head as Sir moves in closer, softly brushing his hard bulge against my leg and causing my skin to prick and my pussy to throb with insatiable need. *Say it now before it's too late!*

My skin flushing a deep scarlet shade, I suck in a deep breath, parting my lips to say the word that will bring me to safety.

Before the first syllable escapes my mouth, he surprises me by suddenly releasing me from my binds.

Immediately, I slump to the cold stone floor covered in sweat, my limbs sore, stinging and red, feeling drained and exhausted, his arm wrapped around my waist and holding me up.

"Are your ankles alright?" he asks me, bending over to massage my wrists, his voice coming out clear.

A feeling of confusion washes over me at the tone of his voice. His demeanor, which was hot and heavy moments before, is replaced by a coolness that makes my skin burn.

He knows you're hiding something, the voice at the back of my head says as my heart pounds wildly within my chest. *And that you were going to safe word him.*

I hate not being able to tell him the truth. But I'm not ready. Not ready to tell him, not ready to lose my V-card, I'm not even ready for a real M/s relationship... or whatever this is.

"Yes," I barely manage with a strained whisper as he helps me to my feet.

My skin stings as he examines me in the places where I was bound, making sure that I have good blood flow to those regions.

My lips part to tell him I'm sorry, that I'm a virgin and not sure if I'm ready, but then I close them. I'm not sure he'll even care to hear my pathetic excuse for denying him. He just seems ready to leave.

And there's no sense in making things worse.

Our session for tonight is over.

CHAPTER 8

Joseph

LILLY'S GONE for the night. And yet again, I feel as though I've scared her off.

It's my own damn fault, but I'm still in shock.

I knew there was an innocence about her; I assumed it was because this lifestyle was new to her. But when my fingers slipped into her tight cunt even deeper, I felt her hymen. I couldn't believe it. How could she keep something like that from me? The look in her eyes told me everything I needed to know.

I stare at the lush carpet as a couple passes me in the halls of Club X, remembering that look on her face. Scared and vulnerable... and raw. She was completely at my mercy in every way.

No wonder she's taking this so slow.

This should ward me off of her. I should stay away for her own good. No matter how much she wants this, the mere fact that she's a virgin is going to make what would be an erotic exploration into something *emotional*. I'm not an idiot. I won't be fooled by the notion that she knows better. If I take this from her, there will be an attachment that can't be undone.

It makes me even more of an asshole that this knowledge only fuels my desire to take her. I fucking wanted her right then and there. The moment I realized... I'm damn proud of my restraint, but my reaction made her run away... again. She'll come back. I won't let her slip through my fingers. Not that easily, anyway.

"Kiersten," I call out to her as she walks through the main hall of Club X.

Her heels are muted on the carpet, and her eyes whip up to me as she purses her lips and searches the empty hall.

"Quiet!" she snaps in a hushed voice, scowling at me and gripping my arm to pull me aside to a darkened corner. It's comical that the sweet little woman thinks she can pull me around, but I let her. After all, she's been a close friend of mine for a lifetime, and at this point, she's the only person I trust.

"That's not my name here." Her voice is low and her eyes dart down the hall again, but it's empty. The theme night has nearly everyone in the dining hall.

A chill goes through my blood. I forget sometimes. "I'm sorry... Madam Lynn." I give her a small smile and she purses her lips, but I know she's not angry with me. She's too forgiving.

"What is it that you want?" she asks, crossing her arms and cocking a brow. I resist the urge to smirk at her. Here she's in control, the Madam of the house. But I know her too well to look at her the way the other members do.

"I wanted to make a Submissive an offer," I clear my throat and tear my eyes away from hers for a moment. When

I look back, confusion is etched on her face, so I continue, "Outside of the auction."

"Oh!" Her posture relaxes slightly, although she remains skeptical. "And what offer is that?"

"A monthly contract outside of the club. I'm willing to split the fees of course. I'm simply not interested in the charade of the auction." I try to make my stance and voice casual, but the reality is that I don't want my flower coming back here. Not until we both know she belongs to me, and every person in this club knows to stay far away from her.

Kiersten raises her brow and I add, "No offense." I don't at all mind giving the Submissive whatever amount she desires, and the club the same. The money goes toward women's shelters. It's a good cause I already donate to, for the same reason Kiersten's chosen it.

It's not about the money. It's about ensuring I'll get exactly what I want.

I've been wanting to take her away from here. I don't have an interest in engaging in activities here, but I want her. I want to break her. That sweetness about her, I crave it. But I covet her tears of desire more. I see the way her back arched as the braided tails of the whip smacked against her skin. The way she touched the marks with a reverence after being lashed. I could show her so much more. I could give her indescribable sensations; things she's never dreamed of. And I want to.

All in time, but not here. She's taking things slowly and going under the radar. I need to take her away now.

"May I ask who?" Kiersten asks with a teasing smile on her lips. She knows exactly who. She's going to take credit for this, I know she will.

"Lilly." My flower.

"I'm sorry Joseph, but the rules are in place for a reason, and Lilly is still finding her limits." Kiersten looks as though she's ready to leave, and if it were anyone else, I'm sure she would. But it's me. So she rocks on her heels, waiting for my response.

I know Lilly is still learning, but she can handle everything I want to give her. She's perfect.

I clench my fists, hating that I'm living by these sets of rules.

Since when did my life revolve around the commands of others?

I've lived my life making demands and seeing that they're met. I've murdered, committed crime after crime and lived a life without consequence. I have more power than any man in this room. More wealth.

I do whatever the fuck I want, when I want it.

But in the last few years, I've simply been biding my time in this empty world I'm living in. I don't feel at all like the man I used to be.

It's time for a distraction. And Lilly is the perfect candidate.

"Don't give me that look," I hear Kiersten's soft voice, laced with sympathy. "I know you're hurting, Joseph," she says just beneath her breath.

I scoff at her. "This has nothing to do with that."

"If you want Lilly, you can approach her and ask to be her Master, although I'm not sure she's ready. If she goes up for auction, you may claim her that way as well. But there will be no deals outside of that." Her voice is strong, although her face is an expression of compassion. I hate it. I hate that she knows me better than I know myself.

A couple's footsteps echo in the hall as she speaks. I concentrate on the patter of the Submissive's bare feet and clacking of her partner's shoes. I'm sick of being here. Surrounded by other people I don't give a fuck about. I want

Lilly where she belongs. In my home, in my bed, *in her cage when she forgets to call me "Sir"*.

"Joseph?"

My eyes snap to Kiersten's, her soft voice bringing me back to the moment.

"Are you sure you should be taking a Slave? Outside of the club, that is?"

My heart sputters in my chest, and my blood runs cold. I know why she's asking. But I'm tired of waiting and living in this limbo. I'm done living by *their* rules. I've never known anything other than the environment I've grown up in, but that doesn't mean I can't care for Lilly. I know I can.

"I'm certain." My words don't convince her, and I know Kiersten's unhappy, but I don't care.

I want Lilly.

And I'm going to take her.

I'm going to *own* her.

CHAPTER 9

Lilly

I BLOW my bangs out of my eyes with a sad sigh as I go through my emails and work documents. I'm trying to make sure that my lesson plans are ready for my new students. My heart breaks when I think about them. They're just middle schoolers, but they've already been through so much. I've read over each and every one of their files, and I can't believe what they've lived through at such a young age. Some of the kids already have a record, some of them coming from families so abusive that it makes me wish that I could take these kids away from their shitty parents.

My pen taps on the desk as I go through each study plan, making sure that they all draw from everything I've learned in these classes. I try to make them as perfect as possible for the kids, hoping that they'll take something from it that helps them. If it can change even one student's life, it will make me happy. I want each and every child to have a chance at a good life, no matter how hard their upbringing, no matter how terrible their circumstances. Just like I did.

A knock at the door pulls me out of my thoughts. I twist in my seat, looking at the door and wondering who it could be. I'm new in this city and I don't really have any friends other than classmates, but all of them are busy right now, most of them home for the winter break. I know it can't be one of them at my door. No one here even knows where I live. *It's probably a package or a neighbor*, I think as I scoot the chair back from the desk.

It makes me wish I was home with my family. But I only have my father, and now that he's remarried, we've lost touch. I know he still loves me, and I still love him, but I don't want to intrude on his new relationship and family. My birthday's coming up soon, and I know he'll be thinking about me. I smile at the thought. He always manages to send me something nice and sweet. Something from the heart.

I at least need to call him, to let him know I'm doing fine.

I make a mental note to give him a ring as I open the front door. There's a white box with an elegant bow on top sitting on the ground outside.

Sir? My heart does a backflip, and the small smile grows on my face. It can only be from him.

Arching a brow and sinking my teeth into my bottom lip to keep the smile from growing, I pick it up and bring it inside to the kitchen table.

I can't wait to open it. He's been all I can think about, although my thoughts have been a confusing mix with me being a bundle of nerves and insecurities. I suck in a breath when I open it and see what's inside.

Several white roses, and a smartphone with a platinum cover on it. My heart pounds in my chest as I pick it up out of the box, examining the high quality finish. A phone? *He could have just asked for my number!* I shake my head at the thought, but my heart won't stop beating erratically and my head won't stop shaking.

I place my fingers against my throat as I stare at the sparkling phone. I'm not sure why he would get me a phone. It's gorgeous, and more than what I could ever hope for or afford, but I already have one. It seems like such an awful waste of money, even for someone rich.

I'm shocked that Sir got me this and sent me flowers, especially after the way we left things yesterday, with me turning him down. I wasn't sure he'd want to see me again. I thought I'd ruined it all.

Maybe there's something really there. God, my heart. I stare down at the roses, gently petting the petals and inhaling their floral scent.

I'm about to close the box, when I notice a note at the bottom with a phone number and several words scribbled on it in a smooth font, a strong masculine one. It's definitely his handwriting.

If you need me, you can reach me here.
  Sir.

My breath quickens as I stare at the words, my pulse racing inside of my chest and my knees going a little weak. I know that I should just box this and put it away, that this may have gone a little bit too far. But I want more... of whatever this is. I hate it. It feels like I'm getting ahead of myself, like I'm running straight into trouble. I've never had a relationship that lasted more than a few weeks. I'm always the one to send them away, not wanting them to get too close to me.

But this isn't like that, is it? I want him to get close. I'm practically haunted by the thought of him almost taking me against the cross. He could have. I was bound and there for him. The very thought sends shivers down my back.

Whatever this is between me and Sir, doesn't have to be anything more than what I want it to be. It can just be the fantasy I've always wanted to explore. It doesn't have to go any further than that. It doesn't have to be *real*. ...although I'm starting to think I want more than a fantasy.

The air fills with the ringtone on my real cell, going off across the room and pulling me out of my thoughts.

I set the note down and walk back to my desk, trying to calm the mix of emotions as I answer the phone absent-mindedly.

"'Hello?"

"Miss Wade?" a woman asks on the other end.

"Yes?" I furrow my brow, wondering what this could be about.

"This is Sarah Parker with Parks and Recreation."

My heart drops in my chest as I realize this is about Zach. That's the only explanation. I pulled every string I could to get his public service moved. I lean slightly against the chair, my hand resting on the back as I lower myself down into the seat. "Yes?" I ask again cautiously.

"I'm calling because Zach White didn't show up for his service today. And he had you listed as his contact." I nod my head, my throat closing and my eyes shut tight.

"Oh," I finally manage to say, disappointment lacing my reply.

There's a slight pause before the woman continues. "I just wanted to let you know that I'm going to have to give a call to his parole officer."

Anger rips my chest as I force out my words. "Okay, thank you for letting me know. I'll try to get a hold of him." I'm so pissed at him. I'm upset, but more than anything, I'm angry. Why couldn't he just do this? Why?

"I'm sorry. You have a nice day."

"You, too," I say as the line goes dead.

Feeling the hurt spread through my chest, I turn in my seat and face the laptop. I need to email Zach and try to talk some sense into this boy's head. It really pisses me off that he wasn't there today. I thought he was really going to try. He told me he would. He told me he was grateful. Some gratitude.

Muttering angrily under my breath, I open my inbox, but before I can start drafting an email, I see a message pop up.

To: Ms. Wade
  From: Zach White

Hey don't be mad at me

I know ur gonna be pissed at me and think I'm lying but i wasnt able 2 show up to my community service because I cut my hand really bad and ended up in the hospital. Then I went home and caught a fever. If you can call my parole officer and tell him what's up? My cell doesn't work and the land line is dead.

Thank u
  Zach

"Oh Zach, how I want to murder you," I practically growl as I finish reading his message. I'm not sure that I even believe him. I grit my teeth, trying to decide what the right move to make is. I remember the way he was in class. The way he tried. He was honest with me then. I nod my head, remembering the days where he really put forth effort. He is a good kid. I know he is. I'm going to call his parole officer and try to smooth things over.

I pick up my cell and dial the officer's number. No one answers, but I leave a message on the voicemail, stating that Zach is going through some things right now and if the officer can please bear with him and not come down too hard on him. He'll be there next time. I let out a frustrated sigh when I hang up the phone, wondering what I should do. After a moment I mutter, "fuck it," grab my coat, and walk out the door. I need to check on Zach. I slam the door shut behind me. I shouldn't go there; this is a job for his parole officer. But I need to really talk some sense into him. And I need to see if he's lying to me and playing me for a fool.

ANXIETY GRIPS my stomach as I roll through the seedy neighborhood, the dilapidated houses making my skin crawl. I don't ever like coming to the south side of town. It's known for its gangs, drugs, violence and prostitutes. I only come this way if I have to. Or if I care so much about a person that I'm willing to risk my personal safety, like now.

Damn it, Zach, I growl inwardly, trying to calm my frayed nerves.

After passing several rundown townhouses, I turn a corner onto the street Zach lives on, my palms clammy as hell as I grip the steering wheel, my eyes darting around like a cat, looking for any sign of danger. I relax a little after I pass several residences that have decent lawns. The houses look a little better on this street, but I still wouldn't want to be caught walking here after dark.

I drive past several more slightly beat up houses until I see a crowd of kids standing just outside a gated two-story stucco house. I spot Zach almost immediately, his tall figure and platinum blond hair standing out like a sore thumb. They're all out there laughing, some of them smoking weed, while others twist around on skateboards on the cracked concrete. Anger washes over me as I watch Zach laugh at a joke one of the kids cracks as he huffs out a large cloud of smoke from his lips. Both hands are visible. He cut his hand so fucking bad that he had to go to the hospital, but doesn't need a bandage? Yeah, okay. Tears prick my eyes, but I hold onto the anger.

I grip the steering wheel tightly, gritting my teeth as it hits me. He *lied* to me. I knew he probably wasn't telling the truth, but seeing it confirmed before my eyes makes my blood boil.

A part of me wants to jump out of the car and drag him to community service. But he has his own car, and I know he can take himself. He obviously just didn't want to.

I roll up alongside the crowd and several heads turn my way, including Zach's. I give him a look as he spots me, letting him know how much he's pissed me off. He stares back at me for a moment, but makes no move to come toward me. I tap my fingers against the steering wheel, waiting, hoping he will. I'm giving him a chance to come over, apologize and explain himself. To make things right.

But to my absolute surprise, he turns his back to me, pretending as if I'm not even there.

"Zach!" I call out to him and he pauses in his step for a moment, but keeps going.

Shocked, I watch as he walks off with the group of kids, one of them even pointing at me and making some sort of joke that causes Zach to burst out into laughter.

Anger and hurt twist my chest as I watch them walk away, being rowdy and unruly. I know he may not want to seem uncool in front of his friends, but I can't believe Zach would do this. This isn't the kid I know.

I don't know what to do. I want to help this boy, but you can't help someone that doesn't want to be helped. That's what's so hard about this job. It's not easy to turn someone's life around. You can give them the best advice in the world, but if they don't listen or take the initiative, there's nothing you can do.

It's definitely not how I thought it would be when I signed up for this. I thought I would be able to tell children my story, give them a sense of hope, let them know that I was here for them, and everything would be alright.

It's a job that's much harder than I ever thought it would be.

Maybe it will get better with the middle school kids, I tell myself. But deep down, I feel like I'm lying to myself. I shake my head as I sit at the stop sign in my car. I refuse to let Zach give up on himself. I won't stop trying. Even if he doesn't listen. I won't give up on him.

I reach the highway and get on it, flying down the road like a bat out of hell. Shaking my head and biting back tears, I turn the radio on full blast, mindlessly singing along to a pop tune. I don't even slow down when I pass the highway exit that will take me to my townhouse. Instead, I turn onto a highway that will take me to the upscale part of town.

I need a distraction.

And I know exactly where to get it.

CHAPTER 10

Joseph

IT'S private in the dungeon today. Without the crowds of people, the air is chilled. It's perfect for Lilly's training. "Curve your back more." I swish the flogger in the air, and Lilly's eyes are drawn to it as she curves her back, raising her ass beautifully on all fours, and showing me her glistening pussy.

She loves it when I use the flogger. I think it's her favorite.

We've only had three sessions here since I've found out her secret, but each one makes me more and more anxious. I want her out of here, but she doesn't take me up on my offer to play outside of the club. She's always anxious at the end of training. She expects me to want more in return, she expects me to push her for sex. But I haven't, and I won't. Not yet, and not here.

This week, I've been showing up every night, because she has been, too.

I keep forgetting to tell her that she needs to call me before she comes, and ask for permission. Not that she needs to, with the tracker and the phone I gave her. But she needs to start using it. Or else the phone will be useless to her and forgotten. I can't have that, not until we've made different arrangements.

The tails of the flogger gently brush along her back as she crawls on all fours in large circles around me. I can just imagine training her in the study at my house. Her knees would be on lush carpet, rather than this concrete floor. I've already started gathering things for her arrival. She's yet to consent to it though. Every night she comes here, and she obeys every command that I give her. The commands are simple; the tasks at hand are her choice.

I've given her so much control, although she doesn't realize it. I never thought I'd want to give up control, to win her over, but it's becoming addictive. Like a game.

I know she wants a collar more than anything, and I've been hanging it over her head. I see the way her eyes linger on the couples whose Submissives have collars and leashes. She's jealous. I can give that to her, and I want to. I want her to be mine in every way. I have no reason to give it to her here though. No man here would come between us. No one has even tried. They're all aware that she's mine--with, or without a strip of leather around her throat.

And the only bargaining chip I have to get her out of this club is that collar.

"Stop," I tell Lilly, my firm voice echoing off the walls of the empty room, although the command was spoken softly.

Lilly's breathing comes in quicker, and I watch as her pussy clenches. She loves being told what to do. She holds her position easily. She's learned well. Every small mistake that's corrected with the whip or paddle, she's quick to memorize. Not because she doesn't like the sting that travels through her body and the heated pleasure left behind. No, it's not that. It's because she wants to please me. Lilly desires approval.

I can give her that. I want to.

I let the tails of the flogger scratch along the concrete floor so she can hear it. I enjoy it when I tease her like this. Making her wonder what I'll do next. Heightening her anticipation.

"Are you enjoying this, Lilly?" I'm tempted to purchase us a private room upstairs. I could have it fitted with any equipment I need. But it's not the same as being home. And I'm not interested in only having this arrangement within the walls and confines of Club X. I'm holding back so much. For nearly two weeks I've been holding onto this desire for her.

I unbuckle my belt and unbutton my pants as she answers, "I am, Sir." I circle her a few times, lifting the flogger in the air before gently slapping it against her ass. She hardly feels it, although each time her body gently pushes forward; she's expecting more. It's a natural instinct.

I'm conditioning her to be still, to stop expecting my reaction during play. She'll get what I give her. Part of me doesn't want to though. I love this side of her. I love that she's not broken in. I love that I can train her to be exactly what I want her to be. She's a virgin in every way.

I bring the flogger up higher in the air behind her, whirling it to make a perfect circle and landing it directly on her right ass cheek.

Smack! She didn't see it coming. She takes the hit well even though she tenses her body, which I'd rather she didn't do. It creates more pain that's unnecessary, and the point of this isn't to hurt her. It's to elicit a higher threshold of her sense of touch that will intensify her pleasure beyond what I could give her otherwise. She knows this, and she knows better than to tense her body.

"Curve your back!" I give her the command, and she's quick to obey. I slowly crouch in front of her as she catches her breath, recovering from the sting on her backside. My hand wraps around her throat as I talk, my lips just inches from hers. "Don't you dare move." I watch her thighs tremble as she stays in position. With a flick of my wrist, the flogger rips through the air and strikes her along her upper right thigh. It's not a hard blow. I still don't know how much to push her, but more than that, from this angle it's difficult for me to see whether or not the tails of the flogger are only hitting her thigh or whether they're also hitting her pussy. And I sure as fuck don't want to hurt her there.

She gasps and nearly straightens her back, but after her instinctual reaction, she curves her back a little bit more. The tempting curve of her body is gorgeous. I kiss her shoulder as she moans into the air, swaying her hips slightly. "I told you not to move, flower," I say teasingly against her lips.

Quickly moving away from her, I release her throat and bring the flogger behind me, hiding it from her sight. I circle her again, loving the heavy pants spilling from her lips. Her panting is the only sound in the room other than the smacking of my boots against the floor. I take a look at her ass, and her right side is beautifully flushed. Tails of the flogger have left red lines in their place. They've blurred together as the adrenaline and blush of her skin spreads. I smack her again on her left cheek. *Smack*! And again on her right.

Each time she gives me a beautiful cry of pleasure, breathing raggedly between the blows. She doesn't move anymore though. She acts like the good girl I know she is. I continue cracking the whip through the air and landing it on her tender lush ass. Her left side, then her right side, hitting only her cheeks and upper thighs. With her focused on her back, her body is less tense. And the lashings are affecting her as they should.

The natural reaction to move away from the flogger greeting her flesh with a hot sting soon turns to her pushing her ass higher in the air, greeting it eagerly upon impact. Wanting more. And that's when I know she's there.

I place my hand along her heated flesh, massaging her ass and thighs before bending lower to lick the center of her pussy. I suck on her clit, but I don't get her off. She tries to stay still, I know she does, but she shifts her balance and arches her back. I've yet to take pleasure from her while she's learning. But I'm ready to change that.

Her curiosity and being my pet have evolved to a genuine desire and craving of my touch. Last night was the first time she asked me if she could please me. I knew what she meant, but I answered her with a simple fact, "You already are." She didn't press the issue, although she kept her gaze on my hardened cock.

I lick the taste of her from my lips as I stand. She groans slightly in protest, but she's quick to be quiet. She's learned that she'll get hers; I'm good to her, she knows that.

I unzip my pants, pulling out my throbbing cock and stroking it once, and again as I stand in front of her. Her chest rises and falls with heavy quick breaths. She looks up at me through her thick lashes, her baby blues begging me for my cock. She nearly crawls forward, my dick so close to her lips, and her so eager to please me.

"I'd like to be your Master," I tell her with her eyes on my dick, watching me stroke myself.

"You are, Sir," she answers me with a breathy voice full of desperation. Her hips sway again, and her thighs clench. She's so close to getting off. We both know I'm not really her Master though. I want more.

"You've been so good, my flower," I tell her sweetly. "What would you like most right now?"

Her eyes dart to my dick, focusing on it, and then quickly move back up to meet my gaze as she says, "I'd like to suck you off, Sir." She hesitates before saying "suck." She's so innocent. Fuck, it's hard to keep my eyes open and hold back the groan threatening to climb up my throat.

A blush rises to her cheeks, and she shifts slightly in her position. Out of all the things we've done, simply telling me what she wants seems to be the most difficult. She's not very good at voicing her desires. But she'll learn.

A rough chuckle rises from my chest. "Don't worry, my flower, you'll be doing that soon. Is there anything else?" I ask her.

"I want to know your name." She tells me immediately, with no hesitation, no shame, and she holds my eye contact the entire time.

"I'll tell you if you come home with me," I'm quick to answer. Her eyes widen slightly, comprehending what I'm telling her.

She's quiet for a moment, truly giving my request consideration. It's the most she's given me so far. I asked her to come home with me three days ago, and she made it clear that she wasn't ready. I'm tired of waiting. "Would I see your face?" she asks me.

"Yes." Although I've given her the answers I know she wants, she's still hesitant. My heart races, waiting for her answer. *Don't deny me.* I know she wants me, but I also know she's very aware of the fact that she's a virgin. That she's scared to commit so much.

She looks at the ground for a moment before telling me, "I'm scared."

"You should be." I hold her gaze as I tell her, "I want full control, and that's a hard thing to give someone." Her eyes close slowly as she sucks in a breath. The idea turns her on; I've known that from the start. She's smart to be so resistant though. I can't be angry about that. Maybe I shouldn't be so forward, to tell her I want so much. But at least I'm being honest.

"Open your mouth," I tell her after a moment. She keeps her eyes on me as she does what I tell her. "Wider." My own breathing quickens as my body heats at the sight of her curving her back, her wide mouth opens eagerly, waiting to please me. I place the head of my dick just inside her mouth. Only the head. "Suck."

Her mouth closes around the head of my cock, her tongue massaging the underside of the tip. Her hands move along the cement floor as I pull back slightly, desperate to touch me and stroke my length and do everything she can to get me off.

The sight of her so desperate for me makes me crave even more.

I want this whenever the fuck I desire her. I don't want to have to come here. I'm getting sick of it.

She moans around my dick, but I pull away. Leaving her wanting, and falling forward slightly. Worry makes her beautiful eyes seem that much wider. She's concerned she did something wrong. She didn't, but I'm not ready to give her what she wants. I need more from her.

"I want you to come home with me tonight. I don't want to have to come here to see you." I'm completely honest with her.

Her wide eyes stare up at me, flashing with genuine concern. "I'm just not sure if I'm ready," she answers softly with disappointment in her voice.

I need to sweeten the deal. I need to be able to provide her with something that she won't get from coming here.

"I can pay you... two hundred and fifty grand... if you

come with me." My thoughts are on the monthly auction the club hosts when I make her the offer. I know it's a bit lower than what she'd get from the auction, but it was the first number that came to mind. Even if Kiersten disagrees, I don't give a fuck anymore.

But the second the words come from my lips, I regret them. She moves from her position, still sitting in a respectful kneel, but she knows that moving from how I requested her is displeasing.

"I'm not a whore." She doesn't look me in the eyes as she answers me, barely above a murmur. Her chest seems to stutter on her inhale. Fuck.

"It's just an incentive," I say quickly. "It wasn't meant to offend you. I'm fully aware that you are not a whore. And I would never see you as that." I'm quick with my words as my heart races, and my body heats. Fuck!

I crouch in front of her, meeting her eyes and taking her hands in mine, rubbing soothing circles on her wrists. I ignore the fact that she's completely disobeyed me.

I'm that desperate, and I should have known better than to say it the way that I did. "I apologize, my flower." I lean in and kiss her. Her lips are hard at first as she holds onto the anger I've caused her, but then they soften, molding to mine. The tension ebbs from my body. Good girl. *Forgive me.*

"I know leaving here is going to be hard for you," I whisper against her lips, cupping the sides of her face and trying to explain myself. "You deserve to be compensated. Especially with what I want from you."

"It doesn't feel right," she answers calmly; at least she's looking me in the eyes now. The moment is lost between us. I nod my head, my chest feeling tight, disappointment lacing my blood.

I stand, tucking my dick back in and buttoning my pants, feeling like a fucking fool. I reach my hand out for her as I lightly say, "Let's go see the show." I haven't gotten her off yet, but I will. I always do. Especially during the shows. I offer her a tight smile, but what we had was ruined.

Her brow furrows, with concern etched on her face. Her eyes focus on my crotch as she stands and frowns. "I'm sorry," she says and her voice cracks as she realizes that I'm once again not allowing her to please me sexually. Not that she'd want to now anyway.

"You haven't done anything wrong," I answer her honestly. I lead her to the exit as the door to the stairwell opens, taking her away from here, and having no commitment from her to leave yet again.

CHAPTER 11

Lilly

IT WILL DEFINITELY MAKE me a whore, I tell myself over and over again.

I've never read a book where a woman accepted money in exchange for sex and I didn't think she was a whore. So if I'm going to judge myself by that same logic, then that makes me one, too.

If I accept Sir's offer. The key word being "if".

No matter which way I look at it, no matter how it's said, I can't see the offer in a positive light.

Sir called it an incentive, but the wording doesn't matter. You can put lipstick on a pig all you want, but it's still a pig. What he wanted was a contract with me.

And isn't that what prostitution is? A contract between two consenting adults involving sex and money?

Anger burns my throat.

I feel insulted that he would offer to pay me. It cheapened

the experience that I had with him. I don't even know why he felt the need to offer me money. Did he think I was that cheap and could be bought after I rebuffed his advances to take me out of the club?

I bite my thumbnail, remembering the look of want in his eyes. I fucking want him, too.

I'm tempted. The kind of money he was offering could make such a huge difference in my life. I could pay off my student loans, my car payment and stash the remainder of the money away for future investments. There's no shortage of things I could do with that money. And it means I'd get him. I'd get to live out a forbidden desire that keeps me awake late at night.

Do whatever you want with it. It will still mean you're a whore, that annoying voice at the back of my head whispers.

I grit my teeth, angry that I'm even considering his offer. But at the same time, I'm breathless just thinking about it. The very idea of being *paid for* makes my body tingle with excitement and exhilaration. It's something forbidden. And that in and of itself is tempting.

"But I am not a whore," I mutter, closing the textbook on my desk. It's not like I could focus on it anyway.

Every time I'm with him, I feel safe. Even though there's something behind his eyes that scares me, something that warns me away, it's what draws me to him. I know I love the way he turns me on and how he gets me off. I've never experienced anything this sexually intense with anyone. And I think… I bite down on my thumbnail again, staring aimlessly straight ahead, I think I want to give myself to him.

I need to shake this off. I want to just pretend like he never offered, but I know the topic of me going beyond the safety of club acts is going to come up again. Not only that, but he's going to keep withholding himself from me. At first I didn't get what he was doing, but now I know exactly what he's been up to. I should be happy, I get all the rewards of being an obedient pet to him, and I don't have to pleasure him in the least. But I want to. I feel like I *need* to. Even worse, the pit of my stomach sinks as I think I'm failing him. He gives me so much, and I give him nothing. I groan, arching my neck back and staring at the ceiling. Why is this so fucking complicated? Why can't I just be normal?

I flip open my laptop to my document for my book, brushing the hair out of my face and ready to focus on something else, *anything* else. My fingers itch to tap away at the keys and get out all of my frustration by getting lost in the world of romance. I stare at the cursor blinking on the screen of the blank Word document for several moments as I run through the images of me with Sir in my head for inspiration. My breath comes in shallow pants, and my thighs clench. After a moment I close my eyes, place my hands over the keys and begin writing the scene that plays before my eyes.

It's a quarter past eight and I can't get him out of my head. His chiseled, handsome smile, his rock hard abs, and his thick, ten-inch cock. Fuck. He's so sexy. I can't stop thinking about his slicked-back dark hair, or the way he looks at me. His incredible eyes bore into me with an intensity that makes my skin burn with desire. I've never met a man that's looked at me in this way, who's made me feel this way. His hands caress my body, running along every curve, making me feel like a possession. Like he owns me. A soft groan escapes my lips as I feel myself clenching below. I need his hands on me now, caressing me, feeling me. I want to be fucked hard, and...

My eyes pop back open and I suck in a deep breath, pulling my hands off the keys. I was getting carried away with the last passage. I swallow the tightness in my throat, and shift in my seat. I shouldn't be ashamed, it's what some books are about. I place a hand on my chest as my breathing picks up. But I don't want my heroine to come off as an over-sexed horn dog the entire book. At least not hornier than the male lead.

I want this story to be...

I purse my lips, wondering how I can make something that's just about sex... something *more*. The darkness in Sir's eyes immediately come to me. They stare back at me, luring me to write about them. About what happened in his past that made him into the dominating man he is today. I place my elbow on the desk, my pointer tapping on my bottom lip as I wonder if he'll tell me. I imagine my heroine, knowing she'd have the courage to ask. If she met a man like Sir...

What would she do? Chewing my bottom lip, I sit there for a moment and try to come up with something. But all I can think about is how the heroine in my book has the courage and strength that I don't.

After a moment I get up from my seat, deciding to pull inspiration from one of my many romances. The second my ass leaves the seat; I hear a telltale ping. I sag back into the seat, clicking on the email notification that pops up on my screen.

I crinkle my nose at the sender. It's from the director of the counseling department. I wonder what it could be about. My heart jumps as I read the subject line. What the fuck?

From: James Cricket
  To: Lilly Wade

Subject: Notice of Severance

Dear Lilly Wade,

You are receiving this email because you are part of a

counseling internship program that has been defunded by state lawmakers.

Over the last year, the Children in Need Foundation has fought tooth and nail to keep the funding for our program. We realize how important it is that children who are disadvantaged get the help they need so they can get a fair shot at life.

Unfortunately, the city council doesn't agree, and has voted to take away the funds that keep the Children in Need Foundation running.

What this means is that all members working under this program are being terminated forthwith, and you will no longer be employed by the Department of Education. It saddened us deeply to have to send out this message to all our hardworking employees, knowing how much so many of you care about these children, and how you all want to make a difference in their lives.

The world needs more people like you, and the entire Children in Need family wishes you all the best of luck in future employment. Don't hesitate to use us as a reference for any future employers. You will all receive our highest and most glowing recommendations.

In the meantime, we will be doing everything in our power to get funded in the future.

Yours truly,
James Cricket
President & CEO of Children in Need Foundation

My body is like ice as I sit there staring at the screen, numb with shock. I can't believe what I just read. My eyes stop at every word, not wanting to comprehend what's written on the screen. I'm hoping that this is some sort of cruel joke. But when I check the sender address, I know it's real. A pulsing pain hits me out of nowhere in my temples. I wince and seethe in a breath, rubbing my suddenly throbbing temples. Great. Now I have a fucking headache.

I continue to massage my temples, hoping it will all just go away. I just can't get over how sudden this is. I really wasn't expecting it. My heart squeezes in my chest as it really hits me. I just lost my job. I lost my fucking job. And the kids... fuck. The pounding in my head intensifies as I focus on just breathing.

For a while now, I believed that I could depend on this job, that I would remain employed until I was done with school.

Boy, was I dead wrong. Now my entire living situation is in jeopardy if I don't find another job in a reasonable timeframe. I only *just* moved into this place. I lean back in my chair, trying to calm my breathing and get rid of this headache. Tears threaten to form in my eyes, but I won't let them. I won't cry over something like this. I rock back and forth in my chair, taking in soothing breaths like I learned in a yoga class. I will fix this. I will find a way. There's always a way.

I don't know what to do, but I *will* figure out something.

My cell goes off just as I feel like I'm starting to calm down, the shrill beeping making my head throb even more. For a moment I debate on not answering it, but then I think it might be my job calling with some miraculous news, and I jump to answer it.

"Hello?" I answer breathlessly, hope soaring in my chest. It has to be one of the counseling administrators. Please God, let it be.

"Miss Wade?" a deep, authoritative voice that sounds somewhat familiar asks. I narrow my eyes trying to place the voice, but nothing is coming to mind.

I hold in a groan of despair. My left hand rubs the throbbing pain from my head as I keep the phone to my ear, closing my eyes and wishing I would wake up from this nightmare. This isn't my job calling to deliver a fairytale. This is more bad fucking news. I just know it.

"Yes?" I try to keep my voice steady, though I'm inches away from breaking down.

"This is Officer Johnathan Johnson with the Department of Corrections. You left a message on my voicemail the other day for Zach White."

My mouth goes dry, and I'm unable to even put forth the effort for an answer.

"I'm calling to inform you that Zachery White is in jail for committing a third offense." If my laptop wasn't right in front of me, I'd slam my head against the desk. Today is nothing but a cruel joke.

"What was the crime?" I ask, my voice barely above a whisper. My heart sinks in my chest, and my throat closes. The state has a three strikes law. My hand runs down my face as my elbows fall to the desk, my left one hitting the keyboard. I want to shove the whole thing off my desk right now I'm so upset and angry. I'm so emotional and feeling overwhelmed.

"Vandalism. He and several other kids went onto an elderly woman's property and spray painted the side of her house." Officer Johnson snorts a derisive grunt. "They almost gave the woman a heart attack.

I close my eyes, my temples pulsing even harder as I remember the crowd of kids Zach was hanging with. Why couldn't that boy have just gotten in the car and gone with me? It would have gone a long way in helping him, and none of this would've ever happened. I shake my head as my eyes close, and I wish I could go back in time and just grab him. But you can't force people to change. I can't force him to make the right decision. No one can.

Now things are fucked.

A sharp pain lances through my skull. *God.* I definitely don't need any more shit right now.

Officer Johnson obviously hears me sigh and must sense the anger and sadness behind it, because he quickly speaks up. "Don't worry Miss Wade, I'm recommending that he be sent to The Boy's Academy, one of the best juvenile corrections program in the United States. If anything will turn your boy around, this place will. It has an impeccable record."

Officer Johnson sounds very hopeful and upbeat. I suspect it's mainly for my benefit, but I don't share his optimism. I just can't right now. The Academy is a few counties over. Strings will have to be pulled to get him there. It makes me happy though, because it really does have a good reputation. I suck in a breath and try not to cry. I couldn't help him, but maybe they can. I feel like I failed Zach.

"Okay," I say, trying to sound strong, but my voice cracks. "Thank you for calling to tell me, Officer Johnson. I'm going to try to reach out to Zach as soon as I'm able. You have a wonderful day."

"Zach's going to be all right once he's in that program, Miss Wade," Johnathan tries to assure me one last time. "Don't you worry. You'll see."

The line goes dead and my headache seems to increase tenfold, my head pounding like it's stuck in a vice.

Just when I thought things couldn't get any worse, more shit hits the fan. Now I lost my job and probably Zach, all in one day. It makes me sick to my stomach.

I open my eyes to see the email still up on the screen. The one telling me I've been dismissed, and the program doesn't even exist anymore.

I need to find a job. *Fast.* I need to find a way to raise funding for the program. My to-do list just got a lot longer. I need money for my rent, and the bills aren't going to stop coming just because I unfortunately lost my job.

My heart skips a beat as I suddenly remember Sir's offer.

No, I tell myself, shaking my head. *No fucking way. I can't- I won't stoop that low.*

Surely I can find another way to support myself. But every option I can think about requires immense time and work. Time that I may not have.

The offer from Sir is immediate. *Easy.* And more money than I could ever dream of having all at once.

I don't have to be Einstein to know which path I should take.

It doesn't make me feel any better about it though.

Fuck it. It's not like I don't enjoy being with him. Like I haven't been fantasizing about exactly what he offered me.

Sucking in a deep breath, I walk over and grab the phone that Sir gave me. My head pulses even harder, almost as if warning me away as I bring up his number and the text screen.

My heart beats along with my pounding headache as I stare at it. Everything in my mind screams at me to drop the phone, but my hands move of their own accord.

I close my eyes briefly before I tap out the message.

Sir,

How soon can we talk about your offer?

CHAPTER 12

Joseph

KIERSTEN IS SO PISSED. I didn't have to tell her that I was doing exactly what she told me not to. But I did.

I don't know why I bothered, but now I'm looking at all these text messages and avoiding her phone calls. I don't have to explain myself to anyone. The only thing she can do is kick me out of her club. I'm sorry that I've hurt her and that I've broken her rules, but I'm not going to allow her to get in my way of getting what I want.

And I fucking want Lilly.

I rise from my seat at the dining room table at the back of the restaurant as I see the maître d' walk through the aisle with Lilly. I button my jacket as I walk toward them.

She's already checked her coat, at least I assume she has, because the thin lace dress she's wearing would have her freezing outside in the chilly January air. The black fabric clings to her curves and ends just about mid-thigh. What's most striking are her exposed shoulders, the lace straps hanging loosely off her shoulders. She's so tempting. She calls to me like no one else ever has.

She's absolutely breathtaking. Her lips are made up a darker shade of red than I've ever seen them before. Any other makeup she's wearing only emphasizes her natural beauty. Her long blonde hair is pulled into a loose bun, looking slightly messy with her bangs swept to one side.

Lilly sucks in a breath the moment she sees me, and takes a small step back. She's obviously nervous. I nod at the maître d', letting him know he can fuck off as I take Lilly's hand in mine, wrapping my arm around her back. She walks with me, her strides even, but she stares straight ahead. My throat tightens at her distress. I lead her to her seat across from me, pulling out her chair and helping her sit down. She desperately needs the help, she's practically shaking.

I take my seat, eyeing her curiously. The sound of my heart thudding in my chest is getting louder. This isn't starting as I imagined it would.

"Thank you," she says nervously, finally looking me in the eyes.

Her small hands grab the white cloth napkin off the table and she places it in her lap, smoothing it over and she seems to calm slightly. But then her eyes hone in on the stack of papers on the table. Instead of looking eager and excited, she looks uncertain and scared.

This isn't what I anticipated. I didn't know why she finally agreed, but I wasn't expecting her to be so... terrified.

"What's bothering you?" I ask her.

She twists the napkin in her lap nervously and takes a deep breath. Her mouth opens with her eyes still closed, but then she shakes her head, placing an elbow on the table and putting her head in her hand.

She's obviously not all right. I'm not sure what's gotten to her but whatever it is, I don't like it. I've never seen her like this.

I place my hand palm up on the table in front of her. Her eyes open at my words. "I'd like you to tell me now, my flower."

She holds my gaze with her beautiful doe eyes. "I lost my job," she says, and her voice is hoarse.

So it's about money. Maybe it's not a bad thing that I offered to pay after all.

She adds, "The entire department lost funding." Clearing her throat with her eyes on the glass of water in front of her, I watch her break down in front of me. My heart hurts for her.

She shakes her head and swallows thickly, looking past me and at the wall blankly. "So there aren't any more of-" she clears her throat again and takes a sip of water quickly before continuing. "So there aren't any more programs at the schools, and I don't know how to change that or help."

"Funding?" I ask. I can fund whatever the fuck I want. My heart pounds in my chest as my fingers slide down the cold glass of water in front of me. Maybe I can take some of the burden off of her, whatever it is.

"I work with underprivileged kids that have gotten into a little bit of trouble." She takes an unsteady breath, but it seems to calm her. "It's only an internship for now until I finish the last semester of school." She takes a deep breath before adding, "It was both my job and coursework for this past semester until the last two classes are available next semester." Her blue eyes meet mine as she answers the question on the tip of my tongue, "I'll be done in December." She readjusts in her seat and finally places her hand in mine. "I'm sorry. I know that-"

She starts to apologize, but I cut her off. "Don't be sorry," I say and rub the pad of my thumb on the back of her knuckles, giving her hand a comforting squeeze. "So that's what you do?"

She nods her head, a small confirmation coming from her lips. "Yes."

She's nothing like me. She's good and pure, so sweet and innocent. For a moment I consider backing out of this. I could give her the money and move on, continuing what we have at the club, or not.

But I fucking *want* her. And I haven't wanted anyone or anything in a long fucking time. Maybe it makes me an asshole for taking advantage of her and the situation. But I don't give a fuck. It's not like I only offered it now when I know she's in need. I never claimed to be a knight in shining armor. Everyone knows I'm the fucking villain. I push the papers in front of her, letting go of her hand and getting back to the contract. She came here for a reason. I need to strike while she's willing and vulnerable.

"Have a look and see if this is to your liking." As I say the words and look up over Lilly's right shoulder, I catch sight of the waiter holding a decanter of red wine as he returns to pour me a glass. I chose cabernet just before my flower arrived.

Just as Lilly's eyes settle on the papers, his presence startles her; she pulls the papers close to her chest, hiding them from his sight. But it also draws attention to her and to the papers. I hide my smirk behind the goblet of red wine, swirling it gently and inhaling the sweet scent before taking a sip.

I nod at the waiter, letting him know it's to my liking and setting the glass back down. I can't take my eyes off of Lilly as the waiter refills mine first and then fills hers. I can practically hear her heart beating out of her chest. This isn't her simply agreeing to something she's familiar with. She's yet to tell me she's a virgin. I'm not taking this lightly.

Although this isn't an auction at Club X, I'm still taking the same precautions. As the waiter leaves, another comes behind him, setting down a tray of hors d'oeuvres. Arranged neatly on the silver pebbled tray are two of each: mini caviar parfaits, pancetta crisps with goat cheese on thin pear slices, marinated mozzarella with chili and thyme, as well as a variety of olives, soft cheeses, and shaved meats.

I'm not sure what my flower really enjoys eating yet, but I'll be finding out shortly. Lilly's eyes glance to the tray and then back to the waiter, as he turns his back to us, leaving us alone and to our private dinner as I requested. Her eyes don't linger on any of the items on the tray. Instead she sets the contract back down on the table, focusing on each line.

"Would you like to eat first?" I ask her, popping an olive into my mouth.

She gently shakes her head and returns to reading the contract before her eyes widen, realizing what she's done. She looks up at me with slight fear in her eyes as she says, "No thank you, Sir."

I nod my head once, keeping my eyes on hers. She waits with her body stiff before I reply, "I know it's different here, in a new environment." I quickly lick the salt from my fingertips before wiping them on the cloth napkin in my lap, her eyes drawn to my mouth. "It'll be like this when you come home with me. But you'll get used to me being your Master at *all* times, and in *all* settings."

She sucks in a breath, and her eyes cloud with lust as she answers, "Yes, Sir." She maintains my gaze, waiting for me to give her permission to continue reading. Such a good girl. I nod down at the papers in her hands, and say, "Go on."

I have the contract nearly memorized.

Contract to be signed on this day, January 13, 2017,
by the following participants.

Master: Joseph Levi.

Slave: Lilly Wade.

Definition of Master and Slave needs.

The Master requests the Slave to be available to him at all times for any needs he deems suitable.

The Slave requires safety at all times, as well as free periods when her Master deems appropriate. There will be no punishments during these free periods, however, the Slave must continue to respect her position and address her Master appropriately.

Definition of Master and Slave responsibilities.

Lilly Wade agrees to obey Master in all respects with her mind as well as her body. She is also responsible for the use of her safe word, lollipop, when necessary and trusts that her Master will respect the use of that safe word.

She will keep her body available for whatever use her Master deems appropriate at all times.

Joseph Levi may use her body in any manner within the parameters of her safety.

Lilly is responsible for answering any questions from her Master honestly and directly, and will volunteer any information he should know about her physical and emotional condition.

She is not to interpret that as permission to whine and complain. She must always address her Master in a respectful manner.

It is the Master's responsibility to make it clear when a punishment is being given, and why it has occurred.

In public, the Slave will conduct herself in a manner that doesn't call attention to the relationship.

No part of this agreement will interfere with Lilly's
career, her physical or emotional wellbeing.

Of her own free will, Lilly Wade offers herself in
slavery to Master Joseph Levi for the period
beginning on January 14, 2017 at noon, and
ending on February 14, 2017 at noon.

Both parties must also note and acknowledge that
this contract is not legally enforceable. It is a tool
to help guide the relationship, and monetary
gains will be provided to Lilly as compensation
in the form of two hundred and fifty thousand
dollars. Lilly Wade, Slave, may at any time leave
without fear of losing Joseph Levi as her Master
for the duration of the contract. Although in
doing so, may be met with punishment if she is
to return.

With my signature below, I agree to accept and obey
what is detailed and outlined for the contract
noted above.

Slave, Lilly Wade _____ Date_____

Lilly looks up at me hesitantly. "Joseph?" She says my name softly, so sweet coming from her lips. I've always hated my name, but hearing it from her, with that look in her eyes, makes me proud of it.

I clasp my hands on the table and nod once, holding her baby blues firm with my gaze.

She smiles shyly before returning to the contract.

"The terms are negotiable," I say easily, waiting to see if she's comfortable with the amount I blurted out in the dungeon. It's the minimum of what she'd get if she were to go up for auction. I should offer more, but I'd rather keep the opportunity open for me to extend the contract into the next month if I'd like to.

"This contract ends on Valentine's Day." Although it's a statement, Lilly looks at me as though it's a question.

"Yes," I nod again and say, "It's exactly one month."

I stare deep into her pale blue eyes, willing her to tell me that she's a virgin. It's been days since my fingers have been pressed inside of her tight cunt, but I can still feel her hymen on the tips of my fingers. I know she's untouched, and I expect her to tell me before signing.

She looks like she's going to tell me something, but she doesn't. Instead she returns to the paperwork, but she's not reading it. Her eyes are focused on the line she's supposed to sign.

"If you're not comfortable with this…" I hate myself for even giving her an out. But in this moment, I fall victim to the vulnerability in her eyes.

"I want to fuck you," Lilly blurts out, covering her mouth with both hands. Her cheeks brighten with a beautiful blush of embarrassment.

Although her little outburst is adorable, I need to make sure she's ready for this. "But are you ready to be my Slave? To give yourself to me in all things for a month?"

Lilly takes a deep breath and then another, all while staring into my eyes. She nods her head and without speaking a word, she picks up the pen on the table, and signs her name on the line.

CHAPTER 13

Lilly

I BLOW a strand of hair out of my eyes as I pack away another tank top, one thought running through my mind.

It's only one month.

It's something I've been telling myself all morning to make myself feel better about accepting the money. That, along with, *after thirty days, I'll be free.* The words are helping some, but not totally alleviating my anxiety about the contract. I went over every single line of it several times. It was nothing like the contracts Madam Lynn showed me at the club when I first came. There weren't any specific boxes for things I was interested in or uninterested in. There weren't any hard limits or soft limits that were indicated on the last line.

I was agreeing to be his Slave. Period.

My heart skips a beat at the thought, my breath quickening. The whole contract is very much in Joseph's hands. It scares the *shit* out of me, yet at the same time, it turns me on. It's a paradox.

There's something about giving this man total control over me that drives me absolutely wild.

I should be ashamed, but I'm not. I want it.

I want *him*.

It isn't lost on me that I'll be giving him my virginity. My *V-card*. It's not that it's something sacred to me, something that I've been holding on to as long as I can remember. I've just never... been with anyone who's made me want to give it to them. I wasn't waiting until marriage. Just waiting until I found someone who turned me on and wanted me just as much. Joseph is definitely that man.

I hardly know the man, and here I am, knowingly about to give myself away. I shouldn't be doing this. I should know better. At the same time, I can't help but think there's something more between us, something I've never had with anyone else. I toss another tank top into the small pile on my bed.

Or maybe I'm just trying to justify it.

He's so much like one of the heroes in one of my romance novels; handsome, dark, brooding, mysterious and most likely hiding a damaged past that'll pull at your heartstrings. That's part of what draws me to him, how much of a living, breathing fantasy he seems to be.

But I need to remind myself this isn't a fantasy. It's real life. And I've gotten myself into some serious shit. Except it hasn't really sunken in yet. I'm not sure when it will. I'm infatuated with the romanticized version of Joseph.

Even now, my heart flutters at how concerned he seemed with making me feel comfortable with the contract.

I stare at the pile on my bed, remembering how he told me to bring only the things that make me happy. I glance down at my half-stuffed bag, looking to see what I have so far. My most favorite books and a new Kindle I bought that has loads of titles on my to-be read list already downloaded, but I'm still missing a few things.

I glance at my list, and go down the line of things I still need to grab, then go about gathering them.

I grab a small blue pillow that's on my bed that I use to prop up my knees when I'm sleeping and toss it in the duffel bag. Walking into the bathroom, I grab my aromatherapy oils and some cherry bath bombs and stuff them in my small toiletry bag. While I'm in there, I grab some nail polish and my three favorite lace nightgowns that are hanging on the rack. I rub my fingers over the lace; they're not nearly as beautiful as what Sir gifted me, but maybe he'll like them.

My body heats, imagining what he'll say. I close my eyes and stop that train of thought. I walk out of the bathroom with my personal items and I go down my list again, getting anything else I might have left out. Comfortable socks and flannel pajama pants that I wear when I'm really happy are next.

In the kitchen, I grab a box of my favorite homemade tea that I absolutely love and get from the farmers market. I start packing it away, but then pause, wondering if he'll even let me use this. I have to remember. He owns me. I have to do what he says, whether I like it or not. So if he doesn't want me to drink my favorite tea, I can't drink it.

Anxiety twists my stomach as I begin to doubt my decision to sign the contract. I'm not sure if I can make it through thirty days of being told what to do. I like to think that I can, but it might be harder than I imagine.

Even though it's a contract, you can always walk away, that voice in the back of my head whispers.

I shiver at the thought of breaking the terms of our agreement. But if I find that I can't handle the situation, I'll have to.

Pushing away the troublesome thoughts, I finish packing and go through the house, making sure I have everything that makes me happy or feel good. My laptop is the last item on my list. I'm about to pack it away when I decide that I want to check my email one more time before I leave. I've been hoping to hear some good news back from the counseling administration and from a lady that I sent the first two chapters of my novel to.

As soon as I open my inbox, two email notifications pop up. My heart jumps in my chest at the first email.

From: Jenna Ramey
    To: Lilly Wade

Lilly,

I just got done reading the chapters you sent me. And I have to say... I absolutely love them! I love how sensual you made the heroine seem, and how dark and dangerous you made the hero. I think you're definitely on the right path with the story, and you should really explore the hero's dark side. Trust me when I say that you have great potential as a writer. And I look forward to reading your next chapters. If they're good as the first two, you might have a bestseller on your hands!
    Love,
    Jenna

A feeling of warmth flows through my chest as I read Jenna's words. It feels good to get feedback on my work. I've always thought of myself as a crappy writer, and have had horrible confidence in my ability. To actually hear someone say that I have potential fills me with joy and almost brings me to tears. Even if she is just a friend who edits for a publishing company. Still, it means so much to me.

I read Jenna's words over and over, each time feeling a little bit better, until my eyes fall to the next email and my joy dampens slightly.

From: Zachery White
    To: Lilly Wade

Lilly.
    I'm sorry.
    Zach

I stare at his words, trying not to feel anger after getting such a lifting message about my writing. He's sorry? That's all he can say after everything I've tried to do for him? I take a moment, sucking in a deep calming breath, trying to look at the entire situation, rather than being consumed by my immediate feelings.

Zach is going somewhere where he'll be able to turn his life around. What he did before is in the past now. Getting mad over it won't help either of us. My eyes flicker across the one line on the screen again. I should just be relieved he's being given the opportunity at a second chance.

Rising from my seat, I shake off the uneasy feelings and close the laptop, putting it into my travel bag.

I leave the bag on the desk chair, as I go through the house and make sure that I haven't missed anything else.

A whole month away. Of giving myself to someone else. *All of me.*

Is it really worth doing this?

I heard about the auction. It would've paid me more than the amount Joseph offered. I'm fully aware of that. Maybe even three times the amount. Possibly more. I overheard a few of the girls talking about how much the virgins go for. But when I think about how anyone other than Joseph could have put in a higher bid, essentially taking me for their Slave, I don't regret it.

It has to be him. I want it to be Joseph who I give myself to.

Shame burns my cheeks as I think about what I've done. I've sold myself to another human being. For money. I would have been with him in time, without this though. My heart clenches, and the nasty voice in the back of my head whispers, *does that make it any better though?*

I pick up the strap of the bag after zipping it closed, and hoist the heavy thing over my shoulder. The strap immediately digs in. I may have packed too much.

I'll never tell a soul what I've done. I'm ashamed, but this is about more than just me. This money is going to be used for a good cause.

I'm sorry.

I think of Zach's words in his email. I'm sorry, too.

I'll never tell anyone, but as I turn out the lights to my living room, I know I want Joseph. And nothing's going to stop me now.

CHAPTER 14

Joseph

I KNOW that I fucked up the moment that Lilly walks through my front door. Her shoulders are hunched inward as I carry her duffel bags into the foyer, leaving them in the corner of the room.

Her vulnerability is intoxicating. I know it's taking a lot for her to do this, so I'll make today easy. The first few days I'll be gentle with her, and ease her into this lifestyle. I only have her for a month though, and I intend to take full advantage of our time together.

Although it's freezing outside, she wore a beautiful dress that ends above her knees. The hem brushes against her thighs as she walks in, taking off her tweed winter coat and hanging it over the crook of her arm. She shivers slightly as she walks in, holding onto the coat as if it's her anchor.

The chill from outside has made her cheeks a bright red, as well as the tip of her nose. The house is warm and inviting though, the sound of her heels echoing as she walks closer to the hall.

I close the door, my back to her as I imagine all the things I'm going to do to her. She's mine now.

I could bend her over the foyer table right now, I could take her with a bruising force from behind and fuck her like I've been dreaming of doing. I can practically hear her hips banging against the wooden edge of the table. I can see how the trinkets I've gathered from all the places I've traveled would rattle as I pounded her tight cunt, taking her virginity in a swift thrust.

I own her; I can do whatever the fuck I want with her.

I know it would turn her on. I know in the moment she would enjoy it. I would make sure of that. Strumming her clit while I positioned my hips against her ass, shoving my dick deep inside of her over and over again until she screamed out her orgasm.

I clear my throat and the thoughts from my head as I lock the door. The gentle click fills the room and makes her turn on her heels to face me. I ignore all the ways I could claim her as I walk to her, embracing her and planting a small kiss on her cheek.

"It's all right, my flower." I lower my lips to hers, pressing them against her mouth gently.

She pulls away for a moment, pushing her small hand against my chest and breaking away. I don't like it. I don't like her pushing me away at all. That's not what she's here for. My heart races in my chest, and my body stiffens slightly. I'll allow it for the moment. But only until she's comfortable. Only until she fully realizes what this is between us.

"It's different here," she says, her voice small.

I stare at her for a moment, registering what she's said. Different? Looking to my left, I take in the open layout of my home. It's modern and dark. From where we're standing in the foyer, she's easily able to see the kitchen and den.

She focuses on the white marble fireplace on the back wall to the right. It's lined with large rectangles of black slate. Although the stone holds a cold feel to it, the warm coloring of the worn leather loveseat and chair, combined with the lush carpet balance out the room.

I watch her face as her eyes skim across the room, taking in the details. Her curiosity makes the corners of my lips kick up into a smile. She obviously approves.

My home is littered with two things: fireplaces, because I love the atmosphere created by the crackling of wood in the warm glow of a natural fire, and artifacts from the places I've traveled in the last two years. As soon as I could leave my family, I did. And I went as far as away as I could get.

Cigars are my favorite keepsake. There are several boxes, some antiques, holding cigars throughout my home. There are a plethora of maps as well. Mostly hand-drawn ones I've collected from the places I've traveled, mountains I've climbed, taverns I've explored. The other trinket I've collected a mass number of are weapons. A set of bow and arrows are showcased in the den. It's from ancient Greece, and one of my favorites. I never used it for fear of breaking it. Lilly's eyes widen when she catches sight of it. She blinks several times, as if doing so will make it disappear. My fingers itch to take the bow off the wall and let her hold it.

She noticeably swallows. I can practically hear her gulp. I know she's just now registering that she doesn't really *know* me. That she signed a contract handing her freedom over to me. And only now is she even beginning to learn who I really am. I don't like seeing her fear. Especially since she's only just gotten here.

"I think you'll feel better once we discuss things a little more in detail." I let my finger trail down her collarbone, down to her shoulder, pushing the fabric out of my way as I go. I only use my middle finger, my blunt nail scraping along her skin gently. Her eyes close, and her body relaxes under my touch. I've conditioned her to do that.

"For now, I'll allow you to be clothed." I talk softly, my words gentle and caressing. Calming her. "It'll be your first privilege that I'll take away. Do you understand?"

"Yes, Sir," she responds immediately. She's falling into character, so to speak. Remembering how we were inside of the dungeon of Club X. That's most likely what it was to her, *an act*, a character she was playing. But now it's real life. When she's done playing but realizes she can escape, that's when I'll see the real her. The piece that she's kept hidden from me while we played.

"If you disobey me again, then you'll be whipped." Her head falls back slightly at my words, her chest rising with a quickening breath. Again this turns her on; she's used to me giving her pleasure with the whippings. But there's no pleasure and punishment here. She has yet to go through a true punishment.

"Yes, Sir." I take her coat from the crook of her arm and set it on the foyer table behind me before returning back to her. She stands obediently, hands clasped in front of her, waiting for me to give her a command. This is the way she should have been from the start. Waiting and ready for me. That's how she'll always be in this house. I just need to train her. I step closer to her, standing in front of her but not touching. Her fingers twitch, but she stays still. "The third punishment is orgasm denial." I smirk at her as her eyes widen in surprise. "That's something you've yet to experience, isn't it?"

"Yes, Sir... May I ask a question?" She's hesitant and I can understand why, but I need her to know that she can always talk to me. There may be consequences if she speaks to me disrespectfully. But I always want to know what she has to say.

"While you're here you can speak freely. So long as you address me properly."

"How long?" I smile broadly at her question, holding back my laughter. My greedy little flower. My reaction makes her smile, her shoulders relaxing slightly.

"Are you already planning on getting into trouble?" I tease her, my middle finger now running up and down her throat.

"No, Sir." There's still the trace of a smile on her lips.

"Are you so certain that you're going to displease me?" I ask her, my finger pausing on her soft skin.

She takes a moment to swallow before answering again, "No, Sir."

"Your punishment will fit the crime. So the length of your denial depends on what you do."

I have to tell her about the cage. These punishments are for minimal offenses, if she does something out of character. But if she does something to intentionally upset me or disrespect me, then that's where she'll stay. I've seen the way she looks at the cages in the dungeon. The one I have for her is larger. There's curiosity behind her eyes, but it truly is a punishment. Both for her and for me. My hope is that I'll never have to use it, although I imagine with her curiosity she may ask me if she can go in, just to see what it's like. Just to tease me with her being unavailable.

"We have a lot to discuss." I splay my hand on her back, leading her away from the front door and farther into my house, her new home for the next month. "Come. Let me show you your room."

CHAPTER 15

Lilly

LUXURY.

It's the only way I can describe my bedroom when I step inside with Joseph at my side, his eyes on my face, watching for my reaction.

I don't disappoint him. My jaw nearly drops to the floor as I survey the room, my breath catching in my throat.

An amused grin curls the corners of Joseph's lips up as he eyes my stunned look. He knows I'm floored by his impressive wealth, and he's enjoying every second of it. *Pure, unadulterated luxury.*

Seriously, I can hardly believe this will be my bedroom. The rest of the house is amazing and I can't wait to explore it all, but this... I shake my head. This is absolutely gorgeous.

I press a hand to my chest. This room is the stuff dreams are made of. It's large and spacious, contemporary, urban and chic, all in one. The walls are lined with an intricate high-gloss gray paisley wallpaper that literally takes my breath away, and soft lush white carpet that looks and feels like a mink fur coat. I kick my heels off as I let it all sink in.

As I move across the floor, my feet are enveloped by the soft carpet, and a soft sigh escapes my lips at the caress of it against my skin. It feels so good to walk on it. I've never felt anything like it. A large king-size bed with a canopy lies at the back wall, the soft white gossamer curtains billowing out from the gentle air circulating around the room. Above it is a tray ceiling painted a pale blue with a diamond chandelier in the very center.

Directly across from the bed lies an exquisitely shaped white hearth over a grey marble fireplace, with a large white recliner sitting in front of it, adorned with pale blue throw pillows.

I spin around, taking in everything from the crown molding, to the expensive finish of every piece of architecture in the room. With all the white, it really looks like a place of purity. Sweet innocence.

Like my virginity.

I try to push the unwanted thought away, not wanting to think about what the cost of the contract entails.

Then I see them. *The toys.* I shake my head. I must be imagining things.

I close my eyes, and then pop them open. *Nope.* Still there. I don't know how I didn't see them before, but now that I have, I can't *unsee* them.

They're all the color of the room, white and grey, so I guess they blended into the background. But not now. Now, they're all I see.

There are white whips hanging off the end of the bed frame, white riding crops on the wall along with large foreign objects that make me shudder at the thought of what they're used for. I start to walk to them, my hand at my throat, and as I do, I hear and feel Joseph walking behind me. I can hardly breathe. I stop in my tracks, lowering my head and just trying to breathe. This is why I'm here.

I lift my eyes and nearly laugh.

There's even a white cage in the corner of the room and a white bench with white leather straps.

I stare in disbelief, wondering how my eyes could have deceived me so. Here I am, enraptured in the upscale beauty of the room, when it's a goddamn torture chamber! A very nice, plush comfortable-looking one, but a torture chamber nonetheless.

Anxiety twists my stomach as I stare at these objects, knowing what they'll be used for. *How the hell did I get myself into this?*

I look over at Joseph and see his eyes on me. He hasn't said a word since we've walked into the room, content on watching my every move and expression as if trying to read my mind.

I part my lips to ask something, but then close them, my legs feeling weak. I don't trust myself to speak yet.

To hide my anxiety, I walk over to the closet and open it. It's pitch dark inside, and I have to search around for the light switch.

Once again, I have to keep my jaw off the floor.

Fuck. The closet is huge. It has its own island, and tons and tons of space. It's the kind of closet that every girl dreams about. With a ton of rack space to dump the latest trendy pumps on. But I'm surprised to see it mostly stuffed with feminine clothing; corsets, silk and lace lingerie. It looks like they're all my size, too.

After a moment, I turn off the light and leave the closet, walking back into the bedroom, feeling stunned.

Joseph is standing there where I left him, his eyes on me. My heart skips a beat at the hunger I see in them. A growing sense of dread rises from the pit of my stomach. I know what that look means. And I know what I haven't told him.

"This is beautiful," I say quietly, trying to keep my voice steady, not wanting to betray the anxiety twisting my stomach.

An amused twinkle glints in his eyes. "I thought you might like it," he murmurs, his voice husky and confident.

"I don't think I've ever stayed in such a nice room before," I say, and then jokingly add, "Minus the whips, chains and cage of course."

Joseph huffs out an amused chuckle. "Those will have no effect on how well you sleep in that bed. You will find it quite soft, actually." For the first time, he takes his eyes off my face, casting a quick glance over to the corner of the room where the white cage is. "But if you disobey me..." his voice trails off, but I know what he means. It's almost like he's itching to see me in the cage.

I slightly shudder, my nipples pebbling. A part of me thinks I would like the cage. I'm turned on by it. But I think I would only enjoy it for a little while--an hour, maybe two, but definitely not for anything longer than that. The thought of being in it for more than several hours absolutely terrifies me. I clasp my hands in front of my dress, swinging my shoulders back and forth, trying to shake the nervousness that keeps running through my limbs.

Joseph steps forward, sensing my emotions, stopping a few feet from me. He reaches out and places a hand on my shoulder, halting my rocking. I almost groan at his touch, feeling small shocks where his skin touches mine.

Fuck, what this man does to me.

Up close, I'm enveloped by his masculine scent and it calms me, if only slightly. *Jesus*, I love how he smells.

"What's wrong, flower?" he asks me with concern.

I look into his eyes, and my heart flips. The hunger is still there, and it's enough to make my skin prick, my cheeks burning red. I know that it won't be long before that hunger will demand to be sated. I just need to... I swallow thickly. I need to tell him. I know it's going to happen soon.

"Can tonight be different?" I blurt out, my heart skipping a beat and then starting to race.

Joseph's eyes never leave my face. "Can what be different?" he asks, and his voice sounds so deep and low.

My forehead crinkles as I frown. Is he toying with me? He has to know what I mean with the way he's been looking at me since I've got here and that giant bulge in his pants that he's done little to hide.

My cheeks still burning, I gesture at the king-size luxurious bed. "Uh, you know."

A grin plays across his chiseled jawline. "No, in fact I don't."

Okay. Now I know he's toying with me.

I shake my head. "I just always thought... it's silly... but I've always been..." I search for a way to say what I want without giving myself away. "I'd like this to be outside our contract? I just... can we just pretend I'm not your Slave for the first time?"

Joseph shakes his head firmly, and my heart falls into my stomach. "I don't pretend, Lilly."

I search his face for some sign of softening, but his jaw is firm. I don't think I'll convince him. My heart races in my chest. All the ways I've imagined him fucking me have been ruthless. But right now, I don't want that.

"Can you be gentle at first?" I ask hopefully. "Just for tonight."

I see amusement flash in his eyes, but his expression remains flat. "That's not in my nature."

It's hard to keep my face steady and my knees from shaking as I look at him. I don't know what I should do.

I've never had sex before, but now I'm supposed to be able to endure a man his size, who's going to fuck me like a wild animal?

Holy fuck.

I'm just as scared as I am turned on.

More than that, I'm uncertain. I'm about to give away my virginity to a man I've hardly known for more than a few days. The realization nearly makes my head spin.

What the fuck is wrong with me?

My next words come out small and tiny sounding. "Is it going to hurt?"

God, I sound so fucking naive, but I can't help myself. I'm terrified.

Joseph reaches out, gently cupping my cheek. "The only pain I give you will be followed by pleasure."

Oh God. Yes.

I close my eyes, shuddering, hoping to find the strength to endure what's to come. I hear him as he takes a step closer, pushing me with him until the back of my knees hit the bed.

You could always end this, says that annoying voice. *You could just walk away right now.*

I don't get to answer it.

I feel Joseph move closer, invading my private space and pressing his hard body up against me. I want him. I've never known anything else to be as true as that single fact.

Fuck. I feel his hard cock pressing up against my hip.

And *damn*. It feels *SO* big. I take an unsteady breath. It's happening.

His hot lips suddenly press against mine, sending electricity shooting through every one of my nerve endings. I tilt my head back, my lips parting in a sigh, my nipples hardening and my pussy heating with need. The sensation is like nothing I've ever felt, and I feel like I'm being turned into pure liquid honey, ready to melt into him.

"You want me, Lilly?" Joseph stops kissing me to murmur, his hot breath scorching my neck.

I groan, wanting his lips back on me, not wanting the sensation to end. "Yes, Sir," I moan. "Please, Sir."

Even though his lips are at my neck, I can feel his grin, along with his throbbing cock pressing insistently against my pussy.

"Good girl," he whispers. I swallow thickly as he unzips the back of my dress slowly. I can hardly breathe as his hot breath sends chills down my body, his fingers brushing against my shoulders as he pushes my dress down my waist and over my ass. It falls into a pool at my feet.

His fingers tickle around my hips. I knew better than to wear undergarments. I only packed a few for the entire month, although I'm not sure he'll ever let me wear them.

He leaves an open-mouth kiss on the front of my throat, humming with satisfaction as his fingers move to my pussy. I stand still, waiting for any direction he's willing to give me. I can hear the words at the tip of my tongue, begging for me to say them. *Please be gentle with me. I've never done this before.* But instead I say nothing as he grabs my hips and lifts me onto the bed.

A startled gasp is ripped from my throat as my back hits the mattress. My heart races in my chest, beating uncontrollably. I glance up to see him unbuttoning his top button and pulling his dress shirt over his head. His muscles ripple in the soft light.

Holy fuck.

I can't take my eyes off of him as his deft fingers unbuckle his belt, and then the button of his pants. He slowly unzips the slacks, pushing them to the floor and stepping out of them along with his boxers. The only thing I can hear is my hammering heart. I lie as still as I can on top of the bedding. I need to tell him I'm a virgin. But I can't, the words refuse to come out.

He crawls onto the bed and hovers over me. His bulky shoulders make him look even more intimidating than usual. The look in his eyes freezes my body. Possession. Power radiates from his very being. He owns me. It's never been more clear to me that in this very moment. He. Owns. Me.

"Spread your legs for me." His voice is soft as he commands me, and then he gently kisses the edge of my jaw, trailing kisses toward my ear and down my neck. I do as he says, spreading my legs as far as I can. He moves between my thighs, his fingers cupping my pussy once again.

I'm soaking wet, shamelessly soaked for him.

He lays his body so close to mine. Only centimeters away. His forearm to the right of my head braces him as he strokes his cock, and gently pushes the head through my folds.

Tell him! I scream inside my head.

My body heats, and begs me to move. I don't. I lie perfectly still, waiting for him to take from me one thing I can never get back. I've committed to it. Fuck, I hope he can't tell.

"Are you ready for me, Lilly?" he asks with a different tone in his voice. Something I don't recognize. I nod my head quickly, swallowing the lump in my throat. "Are you ready to give me your virginity?" Shock paralyzes me for a moment. My mouth opens and closes, nothing coming out. He nuzzles his nose into the crook of my neck, giving me a moment to realize what he's said. I still can't respond when he kisses me sweetly on the lips. My eyes refuse to close.

"Tell me," he says, then kisses me again before moving away from me slightly to rest his thumb on my bottom lip. "You're ready for me?" he asks me, his eyes moving from my lips to mine. I can't deny the want reflected back at me. The pure desire. I nod my head once and with that simple response, the powerful man towering above me closes his eyes and groans as though I'm torturing him.

"Answer me," he says simply, his eyes still closed as his dick presses into my entrance.

"Yes, Sir." At my answer, he slams into me with a forceful thrust that makes my back bow and my neck arch, pushing my head into the mattress. I instinctively reach for him, my nails digging into his back. A silent scream falls from my lips. It feels like a pinch. A hard fucking pinch, followed by stinging pain.

He stays buried deep inside of me, my tight walls refusing to adjust to his thick girth. It hurts! The stinging pain refuses to dim as he stretches me. My eyes close tight, and my forehead pinches, willing the pain away.

He shushes me in the crook of my neck. His hand gently strokes the curve of my waist as he stays deep inside of me. I want to writhe under him and move away, but he holds me still, planting soft kisses down my neck to my collarbone and then back up my throat. Tears prick my eyes; I didn't think it would hurt like this. My heart isn't even moving. My body is so still, so paralyzed with the shocking pain. Joseph puts his hand between us and rubs my clit as he kisses me.

The sensation quickly morphs into something else. My body relaxes slowly and then tightens as my pussy heats, and tingling stirs in the pit of my stomach. I finally swallow, feeling my muscles ease and the pleasure increasing as the pressure builds.

"Does that feel good, my flower?" Joseph asks me in a low voice. I can only moan an answer at first. His hand moves from my clit as he pulls out of me slightly before pushing all the way back in. Fuck! My legs wrap around his waist, ankles crossing and digging into his ass. When he moves, oh God, when he moves, my sensitive nipples rub against his chest. I need more.

"Yes," I answer in a mere whisper as he pumps his hips again. And then again. Each time he brushes against my clit. The sensation becomes nearly overwhelming. Oh fuck yes. This is what I thought it'd be like. My body heats with a cold sweat breaking out along my skin. It's too much. I can't... I can't.

His fingers wrap around my hip, holding me down as his pace quickens. My nipples harden as goosebumps form over my entire body as a cold sweat breaks out, traveling along every inch of my skin. My nerve endings are on high alert. My forehead pinches as I realize I'm about to cum. My body slams into the bed, Joseph's hard thrusts pushing me higher and higher. I'm so close. I force the words from my lips, "May I-" He cuts me off before I'm able to finish. "Cum freely," Sir says in a voice I've never heard, one laced with desperation, his speed increasing as he races for his own release.

The realization of what I do to him is my undoing. I make him lose control. I throw my head back, the intense sensation running through my body in waves. The first is slow, starting from my stomach and working its way out to each of my limbs, tingling the tips of my fingers.

Before the first is even finished, the next comes crashing through my body and as I feel him cum deep inside of me, the final wave forces me to call out his name, "Joseph!"

My body shakes and trembles. My heart is pounding so loudly I swear he can hear it.

As I try to catch my breath, Joseph slips out of me slowly, hushing me when I wince. I open my eyes to see his shining back at me.

He knew. My breathing comes in slower as he plants a kiss on my lips. I can't close my eyes though.

He knew.

CHAPTER 16

Joseph

It's been a long time since I felt the warmth of a woman in my bed. It's been years. A soft sigh gently spills from Lilly's lips as she nestles into my arm. Her left leg is propped up on top of mine, and every little movement is making my dick even harder.

I own her. I could take her again right now if I wanted. But the sight of her sleeping so soundly is something I never thought I'd want to see as much as I do.

Her hair is a tangled, messy halo of golden locks. Her face is partially buried in the comforter that she has up around her neck. The warmth gives her skin a slight blush. I've seen her naked so many times. Last night I felt her raw, not only in the way I took her, but also in her emotions when she gave me something she can never have back. After I cleaned us up, I held her as a lover should, and I was happy to give her that. She fell asleep in my arms, and that's where she's stayed.

She's at peace and relaxed. It's an odd thing to me, the feelings washing over me as I look at her, something I didn't expect.

"Lilly," I say her name in an even cadence, and her breathing comes to a halt as she readjusts in her sleep, still not waking. I move my arm out from under her, the air feeling cool without her warmth.

Her head falls to the mattress without my support. She gasps, opening her sleepy eyes and bracing herself with both hands on the mattress. I give her a minute to wake and to recognize where she is. The moment she sees me, her pupils dilate with both recognition and desire.

I sit up on my knees, shoving my silk pajama pants down along with my boxers so my cock springs free. My little flower is such a naughty girl. She licks her lips staring at my cock, but she's as still as can be on the mattress as she waits obediently for my command. Such a good girl.

"What are you?" I ask her as I stroke myself from end to end, spreading the moisture over the head of my dick.

She breathes her answer, "Yours." Fuck, hearing her lust-filled voice admitting my claim to her with such pride makes me want her that much more. I reach down, grabbing her by the hair at her nape, fisting it and bringing her lips to my dick.

"Damn right you are," I tell her as her lips slide down my cock and my head brushes against the back of her throat. Fuck! She feels too good. It takes everything in me not to groan out loud and shove deeper down her throat. Although I have a firm grip on her, controlling her if I need to, I let her move at her own pace. She nearly gags on my cock, her wide eyes looking apologetic. I don't give a fuck. Her mouth feels like fucking heaven.

I buck my hips once, feeling her throat stretch around my cock. She takes it, her hands almost reaching up to grip me, but she quickly puts them back down, gripping her thighs. Her eyes water as I pump my hips, forcing her to take more, and holding myself at the back of her throat. Only for a moment, right before pulling out and giving her a moment to catch her breath.

She breathes in deep, keeping her mouth open and ready for more. Fuck, she's too good to be true.

She moans around my dick, loving how I'm using her. She gets on all fours, hollowing her cheeks as she sucks my length, eager to take more. Her tongue massages the underside of my dick and her throat closes around my head as she goes as far as she can, her nose almost reaching the coarse pubic hair. Again she moans and her lips push down, stroking my length as she blows me. She moves her lips all the way to the ridge of the head of my cock. It sends tingles down my spine, my toes curl and I nearly cum just from that sensation.

The tip of her tongue dips into the slit, licking up the small bit of precum that leaked out. She moves her hand up to stroke my dick, and that's what I've been waiting for.

Thank fuck she did it before I came. I'm quick to grab her wrists before she can touch me. I pull out of her mouth, pushing her backward and pinning her down on the mattress. Her eyes flash with fear as I hold her down, staring at her with narrowed eyes.

"Did I tell you that you could touch me?" I ask her, my head tilted. A spark of knowing darts across her blue eyes as she realizes what she's done.

"I'm sorry, Sir," she says as her hips tilt and her upper thighs clench. "I had no right." She gives in so easily, accepting what she's done. My fingers dig into her hip before loosening my hold on her and letting go of her wrist.

"Mistakes will be made," I tell her. "I'll allow you one

warning for now." She stares at me, her breath barely coming in as she waits for her punishment.

I back away from her and her lips part to protest me leaving her, her eyes flashing with worry.

I've kept myself from her for so long, refusing to let her please me. And although it wasn't a punishment then, I'm sure she saw it as just that. But I have no intention of not taking from her every fucking day that she's here. She'll learn that soon enough.

"Get on your hands and knees," I tell her as I sit on my knees, ready to feel her tight cunt wrapped around me again.

She's quick to get into position, turning her body so her ass is the closest thing to me. I grip her hips nearly violently in a bruising hold and pull her quickly toward me, reveling in the sweet gasp that comes from her lips. She curves her back like a good girl. She's trying, I know she is. She's desperate to please me. I take her hair in both of my hands before wrapping it around my wrist, gripping and pulling her hair back slightly.

My fingers play at her wet pussy lips as I look over her body in complete submission to me. "You fucking love this, don't you?"

With her neck arched, her voice comes out in a higher pitch, "Yes, Sir." I nearly slammed myself into her tight cunt to the hilt without waiting for her response, but I stop before doing so after hearing those sweet words. But I already know that I can't.

She's swollen from last night. I spread her lips and see she's red. I'd love to ride her hard and fast, to give her the brutal fuck she truly desires. But instead I ease in slowly.

She feels so good, and I knew she'd feel just like this. Somehow I knew.

I slowly slip deep inside of her, letting her hair relax around my wrist and losing my grip on her. Taking her hips in both of my hands, I bend forward and kiss her neck. Her eyes are closed tight, and her mouth is pressed into a small frown. I know she hurts. My hand slips between her legs to rub her clit. I pull back on her clit slightly, exposing the raw sensitive side and press my middle finger down, rubbing merciless circles against her. Her eyes pop open as her mouth forms a perfect "O".

I stay buried to the hilt until her face softens to show more pleasure than pain. Her pussy strangles my cock as I move deep, sliding in and out of her. My fingers are wrapped around her hips and my stomach presses against her back as I bite down, nipping on her earlobe and making her gasp before I pull nearly all the way back and then slam into her. Her hands slip on the mattress, and she falls forward.

With her small body under mine, I buck my hips over and over. I brace my heavy body with one forearm, my other hand holding her hip and keeping her angled just how I want as she fights under me to control herself. I piston my hips, loving how her pussy spasms around my cock and the sounds of her wet cunt being so brutally fucked filling my ears.

Her cheek presses against the mattress with each blow I give her. Her eyes shut tight, and her teeth sink into her bottom lip. She's holding back her screams of pleasure, her hands fisting the sheet beneath us.

"Let me hear you," I tell her in a strong voice I don't recognize in this moment. I'm so lost in her touch. My heart beats fitfully, and my body heats then freezes with an intense pleasure that radiates outward. I'm so close to losing it. But I want her with me every step of the way.

Her mouth opens instantly, obeying me as I continue my ruthless pace. She screams out my name over and over, not addressing me as Sir but instead calling me Joseph. I wasn't expecting it, just like I wasn't last night, but my name on her lips sends me over the edge. I desperately rub at her clit as thick streams of cum fill her tight pussy.

Her small body shakes under me as her own release finds her. Thank fuck!

My mouth parts as I take in a sharp breath, loving the way her tight cunt strangles my dick.

I brace myself with my forearm, wiping the sweat off my forehead and gently stroking her side, until her body stops trembling and her breathing finally steadies.

My own breathing is coming in heavy as I sit up on my knees. Her small body is lying limp on the bed, her shoulders rising and falling with heavy breaths. Her eyes are wide open, darting from me, back to the bed as she stays still. Her body shivers uncontrollably, but I'm not sure if it's from a chill or from the intense pleasure of her orgasm. As I climb off the bed I grab the edge of the comforter and bring it up to her shoulders.

"Don't go back to sleep now, my flower." I kiss her forehead, loving how she closes her eyes and trembles beneath my comforting touch just as much as she did from the ruthless way I fucked her. I whisper against the shell of her ear, "We're just getting started."

CHAPTER 17

Lilly

I LIE BACK against the mattress, my chest heaving, my pulse racing as I look up into his eyes. God, he's so handsome. I could look at his face all day. He leans in close, his hard body pressing up against my soft skin. Down below, I can feel his hardness pressing up against my stomach. I can feel it throbbing, pulsating along with my heartbeat as he brings his lips against my neck.

A soft sigh escapes my lips as I arch my back against the bed, pressing my body into him.

I want him.

I need him.

I'm just not sure if I'm ready.

He pulls back as if sensing my anxiety, his deep brown eyes searching my face.

"Do you trust me?" he asks softly, his breathing heavy.

I stare back into his concerned gaze, not sure what to say. Do I trust him? I've only known him for a few weeks, and while I am infatuated with him, I'm not sure if I trust him.

At the same time, he's treated me better than anyone else has ever treated me. He's shown more concern about my well-being than anyone ever has. Most of all, I'm sure he's willing to wait until I'm ready.

But I'm not going to make him wait.

Not today.

"Yes," I breathe, my heart in my voice. "I trust you."

His handsome face splits into a grin, his eyes sparkling with happiness. "Good."

As he comes in closer, bringing his lips close to mine, I relax my body and prepare to surrender myself wholly to him...

Smack!

The memory of being spanked jolts me out of the book I'm working on and I pull my fingers back from the keys of my laptop, my breathing ragged. I can still feel the sting of the paddle against my ass. Joseph disciplined me for talking back to him this morning.

At the time, I thought I was being myself and it was all just harmless banter. He even smiled as I was doing it. He played along. My heart warms at the memory.

But I was still *punished.*

Harshly.

My eyes fall down to my naked legs and I see the goose-bumps covering them, the faint red marks my disobedience has earned me. I squeeze my thighs together, feeling my clit pulse, turned on by the sight.

I've lost my clothing privileges, all because I sat incorrectly at the table. Joseph wants me seated with my legs spread if I'm in a chair. His rules are simple and easy, but unnatural. I purse my lips. These punishments aren't really fair. But at the same time, I welcome them. Being bad has never felt so good.

They're erotic, sensual even, and they bring back memories of being whipped in the dungeon.

My nipples pebble, and my pussy clenches around cool air as I think about these *punishments*.

It's been a crazy last few days, and I still can't believe I gave myself to him. Or that he *knew* about my virginity. My fingers tap on the keyboard and I look over my shoulder and out to the hall, shifting on my bed with my laptop balanced on my thighs.

I was concerned I'd regret giving myself to him. But with everything I'm feeling, regret isn't even on the radar. Even when I unknowingly disobey him.

He's taught me so many things in such a short amount of time, gave me pleasure that I'd never dreamt possible. The way he makes me feel, taking my body, ravaging it, devouring it. *Owning it.*

I shake my head, at a loss for words.

I love it.

I love both sides of Joseph. The nice and caring side, and the dominant side. Although, he's been showing the dominant side more these past few days. It seems like he's controlling everything I do or say now. Just this morning he had clothes laid out for me that he wanted me to wear, along with the oils that he wants me to put in my hair. I love the smell of them actually.

And strangely enough, I want more of this. More of his control.

More of him.

Thinking about him makes me wonder what he's doing.

Crawling off the bed, I leave my laptop and go search through the house for him.

I look through several of the rooms, including his bedroom before I find him in his study. He's sitting at his desk, his head down as he writes in a notebook. It looks worn and I tilt my head, narrowing my eyes as I notice the binding is leather. His brow is furrowed; he's clearly focused on whatever he's writing.

I bite my lower lip as I look at him, my heart racing as my hand stills on the doorframe. He looks so gorgeous sitting there in slacks and a white dress shirt opened at the chest. I don't know if I should disturb him. He did tell me that I have permission to come to him at all times, but he looks busy and I don't even remember why I came to find him. I almost turn and leave, twisting on my back heel, but he looks up, freezing me in place.

I step fully into the doorway, clasping my hands out in front of me like he taught me to do, and then I wait patiently.

I don't have to wait long.

"Yes?" he asks in a low voice, slowly setting the pen down. My heart thump, thump, thumps.

Opening a drawer off to the side, he places the notebook into the drawer and then closes it, his eyes on me the entire time.

A feeling of suspicion washes over me at his actions. What was he writing?

Joseph clears his throat and says, "Lilly?"

I stare at him for a moment, noticing for the first time that he looks stressed; something's bothering him.

He's sitting in his chair, tense as can be, worry lines etched in his forehead. I've never seen him like this.

I lick my lips, hesitating to respond. I don't want to say anything now. I'm not here for anything important anyway. I was just coming to play around and do something to get punished, but it all seems so trivial now.

Joseph's going through something.

It's insensitive of me to expect him to stop what he's doing to indulge me. My fingers twist around one another. A strange sense of loneliness washes through me.

I think back to the hero that I'm writing about, with his dark hair and dark eyes, and how much he reminds me of Joseph.

"Flower," he growls warningly, his deep voice pricking my skin.

Shit. I have to say something now.

"I was hoping I could please you, Sir," I say softly. The moment the words leave my lips, I regret them. Looking at him, I know that he's not in the mood for playing.

His pause hurts almost as much as his next words. "Not right now."

I was expecting it, but it still hurts, a heavy weight settling on my chest. I try to turn away quickly before my face crumples into a frown, intent on running back to my room and closing the door behind me. I don't make it two steps before he calls me back to him.

"Come here," he commands me. "Now."

I bite my lower lip, holding back tears, and turn on my heel and make my way over to his desk to stand beside him. I don't know why I'm so emotional. But something about this moment is off.

He looks up at me, a sadness in his eyes that tugs at my heartstrings. "Kneel," he commands.

I obey his command immediately, sinking to my knees beside him. Swallowing, I look up at him, not sure if he's going to punish me, scold me, or both.

I startle when he reaches out and pets my hair softly. "You've been a good girl," he tells me. "You can put your clothes back on if you'd like."

My heart drops in my chest. I don't want to put my clothes back on. I want him to take me. *Punish me.* Anything.

"Okay," I say, rising to my feet, my throat closing. I try to hide my displeasure, but I can't keep the frown off of my face. I wish I could just disappear.

Anger sparks in Joseph's eyes. "I didn't tell you to get up," he growls, his deep voice low and dangerous.

My heart skips a beat and then starts racing, excitement coursing through my limbs. Maybe he will punish me after all.

I cross my arms over my breasts and try to think of something smart to say. But before I can say a word, he jumps up to his feet and grabs me by the wrist.

"I can see exactly what you're doing," he says in a calm, controlled voice. "I don't want you to deliberately disappoint me, do you understand?"

I stare into his eyes, my heart pounding. There's anger there, but a different kind. One that isn't attached to sexual emotion. I hate it. I hate that he's making me feel this way, like I've done something so horrible to turn him off.

"I wasn't trying to do anything-" I begin.

"Don't lie to me, Lilly," he growls, cutting me off. My heart clenches. I don't like this. I want to go back in time five minutes and never have stepped in here.

I square my shoulders, and rather than tell him how I'm feeling, how I'm craving his punishment in the pleasure that he gives me, and how I hate that he's in whatever mood he's in right now, I snap, "I don't know what you're talking about."

His grip tightens on my wrist, his eyes narrowing. I can tell he's pissed off that I won't tell him the truth. But fuck him. I don't have to give in to him when he doesn't give in to me.

His next words are cold and harsh. "Stop denying it."

Anger tightens my chest at his threat. All I wanted was to have a little playful fun, get each other off. It's not my fault that I'm begging for sex. He did this to me. He made me want it. He made me need it.

Need him.

Even now, I'm breathless with desire as he stares at me angrily, his lower jaw bulging out from being clenched tightly. But he doesn't want me right now. And that pisses me the fuck off.

Too angry to speak, I raise my chin in defiance, letting him know that I'm not going to do what he wants. He can fucking punish me.

That's when something inside of him seems to snap and he pulls me into him with great force, causing me to cry out in shock.

Next thing I know, his powerful fingers are wrapped around my chin, forcing me to look into his eyes. My blood turns to ice as I look into them, and for the first time that I've been with him, I feel very real fear.

There's darkness there. A cold emptiness that makes a chill shoot down my spine.

I don't know this man. Or what he's truly capable of.

And that terrifies me.

The next thing he says frightens me even more, his voice low and very dangerous sounding.

"Go to your cage."

CHAPTER 18

Joseph

SHE THINKS SHE KNOWS EVERYTHING, and I've been pushing her to find her boundaries. To find that breaking point where she'll realize she isn't getting what she wants. So far, she's wanted to obey me. And every command she's met head-on. The perfect slave.

I knew at some point she'd break. I knew I'd ask too much of her. I imagined it would be something much more than simply not telling me that she's deliberately disobeying me. She's always had a problem expressing herself though, so I shouldn't be as shocked as I am.

I can read her so easily. I know she was disappointed. But this relationship isn't me being available to her. It's her being available to me. I'm restless in the leather armchair in the living room, her laptop on my knees as I read through the scene she's been writing. I've given her permission to write every day. When she feels the inspiration, she can do so. I huff a humorless laugh. I've given her permission to do whatever the fuck she'd like when my dick isn't in her. Maybe that was my first mistake. It's my fault she's in the cage.

I take a small sip of the whiskey before sitting the glass back down on the end table.

I scroll through her scene, reading about the collar the hero has given the heroine. She's romanticized everything. Her perception of what this lifestyle is, is missing an important aspect. The one where I have control.

This is why I didn't want a Submissive. My fingers tap on the short glass in my hand before bringing it to my lips again. I didn't anticipate that the boundary that would send her to the cage would be refusing to tell me the truth.

I thought better of her than that. Of everything I've asked her to do, that seems to be the least difficult. But maybe she doesn't want to believe it herself.

My eyes read over the next scene she's written, the hero of her book taking the virginity of the heroine. It's not difficult to see that it was inspired by how I took her. This hero kisses her sweetly, talks to her gently. He *makes love* to her.

This man is nothing like me. The stark contrast reminds me of where I came from.

I remember the first time I saw my father kiss my mother. She was always quiet. Always in the background and never allowed to be around us. I didn't quite understand it. She wasn't allowed to interfere, that's what my father told us.

She approached him, her eyes wide with worry as she talked in quiet whispers, pleading with him for something. Her eyes kept darting toward us as we sat on the floor of the living room, cleaning the guns.

My father was rough with her. I watched as he grabbed the back of her hair so tightly he ripped some out. He kissed her hard on the lips, smearing her lipstick across her face before throwing her down on the ground. I remember how I jumped up, how my heart raced in my chest. I knew how hard my father hit, all too well. She landed hard, wincing with pain as she braced herself.

But the look on her face changed when she saw me watching, slowly walking toward them. She shook her head, her eyes warning me to stay away.

That was what we had as an example. It sickened me. I loved my mother, and I couldn't watch as my father hit her. Day in and day out, she became an outlet for his anger. As my mother whimpered on the floor, I looked back to my brother. Wanting to make sure he was all right. We were only children. But the look in his eyes sickened me. It still does. The smile on his face showed what kind of a man he would be. If you can even call that a man.

That's the day I realized that my father was a sick fuck, and the cold dark look was echoed in my brother's eyes.

I down the whiskey and close the laptop at the unpleasant memory, setting it on the ottoman and rising from my seat. I ignore the fact that I feel like an asshole. I'm fully aware that she's under a different impression of what this is. She shouldn't be. It's my fault, and I need to fix this.

I look at the clock and see it's been an hour. The time has passed by slowly; tick-tock, tick-tock. I wanted to go to her every minute that she's been in there, but she needs to learn she can't top from the bottom. I'm the one with control, and she won't force my hand to get what she wants.

All the punishment she's received up to this moment has been for conditioning. The punishment was to help her learn how to please me. Although there's pain, it's always been accompanied by far more pleasure. She takes a simple punishment, and then she's rewarded for accepting it.

Not this time.

Hopefully this will be the last time. But I doubt it will be. There is a ferocity in her. A strength that she doesn't recognize. She may not know how courageous she is, but when most people see me, they cower. She was drawn to my power. That in and of itself shows courage.

My blood rushes in my ears, and my body heats as I move to her room. I open the door slowly, peeking in to see her curled in a ball on the floor of the cage. The cage itself is large enough for her to stand. I imagined her in the corner with her knees tucked under her chin, her arms wrapped around her legs.

And that's just how she is.

She peeks up over her knees as I close the door.

Her eyes are red-rimmed. She's been crying. Seeing her like this hurts me.

"Are you ready to behave?" I ask her, slowly walking toward the corner of the room. The cage door is slightly ajar; I didn't lock it, but I know she didn't leave it. It's not in her nature.

She can leave if she wants. At any time, she could go and break the contract. But she doesn't truly want to leave. She wants to fight me; she wants me to earn her submission.

And I fucking love the challenge.

This part of it though, I'm not sure I want to do again. I'd rather fuck her into submission.

I crouch in front of the cage, opening the door all the way. She watches me with wide eyes. When the door creaks open, her body stiffens as she says, "I didn't unlock it." I stare back at her as she continues, her voice soft. "I think you forgot to lock it, Sir."

"Did you leave?" I ask as I sit on the floor with my legs crossed. I already know she didn't. She shakes her head and whispers, "No."

"I didn't forget anything, my flower." I pat my lap, waiting for her to crawl out to me. "I'll never lock you in here. It's in our contract."

She seems hesitant for a moment, her movements stuttering.

"You did read what you signed, didn't you?" My voice comes out playful. I know she read every word more than once. I know she takes it seriously. Her lips show the trace of a smile, but it quickly disappears as she wipes away the tears under her eyes.

"Yes, Sir," she answers beneath her breath as she crawls out. She doesn't hesitate to come to me, nestling herself in my lap and resting her cheek against my chest. I comfort her, rubbing her back with firm strokes.

"You know I had to punish you, don't you?" I ask her.

She nods her head against my chest as her fingers intertwine nervously. "I do." She clears her throat and says, "I'm sorry, Sir, I shouldn't have lied to you. I shouldn't have tried to push you."

I kiss her hair, petting her as she apologizes. I hate this. It's something I knew that was going to happen, but I didn't expect my reaction. Or hers.

"I-" I clear my throat and shuffle her in my lap. I don't mind that she came to me. I'm dealing with my fuckface of a brother. He wants the money back. The money they planted on me to set me up. He's trying to get me back under the *familia's* thumb. It's not going to happen. "I will attend to you when I can. But sometimes you have to wait."

Lilly nods her head diligently.

I hook my finger under her chin, and look her in the eyes as I tell her, "Trust me, I would have much rather been spending time with you."

I kiss her, the taste of her tears touching the tip of my tongue as she gives into me, parting her lips. Her eyes are still glassed over with unshed tears. I brush my thumb along her cheek, and kiss her again. I say the only words I know that will make her smile again.

I brush my nose against hers and say, "I think you need to be punished, my flower."

I KNOT the rope at her wrists, tying them tighter. Her lips part, gifting me that beautiful sound.

Testing the give of the rope, I pull slightly, her small body falling forward. She's on her ass on the floor. Naked and waiting for me to command her.

I'm running out of these stupid rules. It's not about training her anymore, it's about pushing her limits and simply enjoying each other's touch.

I pull her closer to me, her arms bending as my lips brush against hers. My heart seems to slow when I open my eyes and find her pale blue gaze shining back at me. There's a look there I should fear. Something that tells me I should end this. But I don't want to. I refuse to.

CHAPTER 19

Lilly

I LET OUT A GROAN, rubbing soothing circles on my right ass cheek as I stop in the hallway outside of Joseph's room.

I'm sore all over. From being used. Deliciously used. But I need more of whatever it is he rubs on my ass after he's done spanking me.

Over the past several days, Joseph's given me nothing but sessions of rough, pleasurable sex. At this point, I can't tell if I'm aching from one of his spankings or his thick cock. I smile at the memory of this morning. No doubt the spanking when it comes to my ass.

It's a good problem to have. And I could definitely learn to love it. I just wish I didn't feel it right now. It's getting in the way of my snooping. A mischievous grin slips into place. I know I'm being a bit bad, but technically there's no rule against it.

For the past hour, I've been looking around the house,

trying to figure out what Joseph's hiding. I *know* he's hiding something. A part of me is scared to find out. And the other part of me is hoping that I'm just being paranoid. I bite down on the inside of my cheek. He won't tell me about his past. Or whatever the hell makes him hide away in his study. I'm sure as fuck not gonna sit around waiting.

The wooden floor creaks in the hallway under my weight the second I slip out of my room. Dammit. I'm not the best at being quiet. My heart stills and I stand frozen in the hallway, glaring at the wooden floorboards. After a moment, I straighten and continue on into his room. I practically tiptoe, my tongue stuck between my teeth as I sneak into his room. I love it in here. It's so... him.

Furtively I look around, wondering where I should start first, my heart pounding in my chest. I don't have much time. I don't know when Joseph will come out of his study, so I need to move quickly. I should hear him, I keep telling myself. I will definitely hear him when he comes up the stairs.

I purse my lips as I walk over to his dresser and start digging through it. I go through five drawers, but don't find anything but neatly folded clothes. Where else do people hide shit? I figured the dresser would be a gold mine. That's where I hide all my shit. I shut the last drawer gently, feeling a little let down. I look up and spot his bed, a smile curling on my lips. *The mattress.* I search underneath the bed and then push my hand below the mattress, between the box spring and the frame. I'm weak as shit, and holding it up actually makes me winded. *Nothing.*

"Come on," I mutter, looking around the room frantically, "Everyone hides something under the mattress."

I get down on my hands and knees and look under the bed again. He's gotta have something somewhere.

I search the nightstands. Nothing again.

Frustrated, I stop and place my hands on my hips, biting my lower lip and thinking.

If I had a big house like this, would I hide anything in my bedroom? I mean, how stupid would that be? Maybe I'm in the wrong room. I sure as fuck can't search his study though. Not while he's in there at least.

I'm about to give up and leave the room when my eyes fall on the closet. The door is slightly ajar, and the light is on inside. My pulse picks up speed as I stare at it. I don't know how I didn't notice it already. I used to hide in the closets. The thought makes my heart hurt.

It's where I found my mother. I think she wanted me to find her before my father did.

He used to tell me how much I looked like her, until she killed herself. Then I would see that pained look in his eyes, and I knew it was what he was thinking, but he never said it again.

I know that's why he doesn't see me much; I remind him of her. I know it hurts him. I understand it. He still loves me, and I love him. Even if our family is scarred from what my mother did.

I bite my lower lip, shoving the sad memory back where it belongs, in the past, debating on whether I should go digging around more. I've already been looking for the past half hour, and Joseph doesn't spend very long on his own.

I should leave, I tell myself. *I'm not going to find anything in there anyway.*

I start to walk out of the room, but when I reach the doorway, I can't bring myself to leave without at least checking the closet. Though I know I probably won't find anything, who knows when I'll have another chance like this?

I spin around on my heel and walk quickly to the closet, swinging the door wide as I walk inside. It bangs against the wall, and I wince at the sound. I don't think he'll hear it though. Damn my eager ass.

Not wasting a second, I quickly go about inspecting the large closet, but I have to pause to suck in a sharp breath at the sight before me. *Jesus Christ.* He has *so* many suits. And they all look so fucking expensive. Who owns suits like these? I want to run my hands down all of the fine clothing, but I'm not here to look at his wardrobe. Focus, Lilly!

I go through several of the suits, checking in all the pockets, looking for something, anything that will tell me something about the past I feel Joseph is hiding. I come up empty. I look around, looking for a safe, some sort of bag, anything where something can be hidden. But I don't see a damn thing.

I'm about to leave the room when my eyes fall on a shoe box that's sitting inconspicuously next to a row of shoes. Looking at it, I know it's probably just shoes in there, but I can't help myself. I rush forward, nearly tripping to get to the box, and grab it. My heart stutters in my chest at the bit of racket I'm making. I only need one more minute.

Yes! Finally! There's a leather-bound book inside with a worn gold latch. I take it out, marveling at the high quality feel.

I open it, quickly glancing over my shoulder as I sit on the floor of his closet, to see pages filled with neat handwriting. One name keeps popping up off the page; *Passerotto.* I say it over and over again, whispering under my breath. I don't know what it means. I have no idea, but it definitely sounds Italian. I try to read some of the entries, and it's hard to keep up, but there's a lot mentioning of the *familia.* What the hell? Joseph is part of the Mafia? My heart beats faster, and my anxiety starts to grow.

I read a little bit further and find out that he's left *the family,* but it doesn't give me any relief. I scan an entry, my heart breaking in my chest. He watched his mother being beaten. He didn't do anything. I can tell by the way he's written it, he blames himself.

I get several more paragraphs in, so absorbed in the moment that I forget the time and where I am. I can feel my heart breaking as tears cloud my eyes. *Joseph*. I can't believe what he's been through.

A loud sound of footsteps coming up the stairs pulls my gaze from the pages of the book and a curse spills from my lips, "Oh shit!" I throw the book back into the shoe box and quickly set it back in its original place.

I'm about to run from the room when I knock over several suits on the clothing rack. My clumsy ass. Dammit. I'm the worst at this. Crap. I bend over to pick them up, but a metal glint catches my eye.

Holy fuck.

My heart jumps in my chest at the sight before me. A gun rack, hidden behind the fallen suits. It's filled with all sorts of guns.

"Tsk tsk," says a deep voice from the closet doorway.

I spin around, my heart pounding in my chest to see Joseph leaning against the doorjamb, gazing at me with amusement. I swear my heart wants to run away, and it chooses to try by climbing up my throat.

"Bad girl, my flower," he says playfully, a twinkle in his eye.

My heart is beating so fast it feels like it's about to burst out of my chest. I know I will be punished for this. And I know it will be the cage. I try desperately to come up with an excuse. Something. Anything. But I'm in his closet.

"Please sir," I plead, holding my hands out imploringly, "I was just looking around –" My throat is so dry as I speak. My body is tingling with fear.

"It's all right, flower," he says easily, surprising me. My

heart doesn't believe him though, and it's still fighting to leave my body, ruled by fear. "There's nothing wrong with you having a little look. I want you to feel comfortable here."

"I'm sorry sir," I say softly, relief slowly coursing through my blood.

Joseph motions at me. "Come here."

I look down at his suits that are on the floor, swallowing and bend to pick them up, but Joseph stops me with a terse, "Now."

That tone he uses makes me walk to him immediately, cringing as I step around his expensive suits left on the floor. He leads me back into the bedroom, pulling me by the hand and sitting me down on the bed. Gazing into my eyes, he gently strokes the side of my cheek, making my skin prickle all up and down my arms. I can still hardly breathe. I'm waiting for the other foot to drop, waiting for a punishment or admonishment. I knew what I was doing was bad. ...I also know I'm not really sorry. I'm only sorry I got caught. And I bet he knows that, too.

"There's nothing to be sorry about, flower," he tells me softly as if reading my mind. He pauses, and then gives me a playful nudge with his nose. "Unless you want to be sorry that you weren't waiting on my bed for me, naked with your legs spread wide."

A smile spreads across my face, and I let out a girlish giggle at his playful words. I really love these moments, when his playful side shines through. It's so different from the dark, dominating Master side. And I want more of it. I cup his face in my hand, looking deep into his eyes and rubbing my thumb across his stubble.

"I like you like this," I say softly, still not quite sure if he's really not mad at me. Maybe he knew I'd be looking. He always seems to know what I'm up to.

"Like what?" Joseph asks.

"I don't know, just when you're kind and playful."

He scoffs, shaking his head as he responds, "Those words aren't used to describe me very often."

"I really like this side of you," I say, placing my hand on his. A moment of silence falls over us, and I feel compelled to ask, *"Passerotto?"* I'm not sure if I pronounced it correctly. Or if me prodding is going to tip him to the point of being pissed off. But I want to talk. It's in my nature.

Joseph hesitates for a moment, and I fear he might close himself off. But instead he grabs onto my waist and pulls me onto his lap. I gasp and hold onto him, not expecting it. He seems to pull me into his lap whenever we "talk." I like it. Yet another thing to add to my Things-I-Like-About-Joseph-Levi-list. I nestle into his lap and wait patiently.

"Yes. It means little sparrow."

"Who did that journal belong to?" I ask, although I'm certain it's his.

"My mother gave it to me when I was little…" Joseph's eyes are distant as his voice trails off. I place my cheek on his hot chest, listening to his heart and playing with the smattering of chest hair peeking through his unbuttoned shirt. I can sense that this is something he doesn't want to talk about, but I don't want to lose the opportunity to get him to open up.

"Go on… Please," I say very softly, stroking his hand and pulling away from him enough to look him in the eyes.

Joseph swallows audibly. But I'm pleased when he continues speaking. "I don't like talking about my past, but you seem to make me talk, my flower. I've had a fucked up life. There were a lot of times where I thought I wouldn't make it after the shit I had been through, after the shit I seen." He runs a hand down his face and looks past me.

The pain in his words pulls at my heartstrings.

"What did you see?" I ask, my voice barely above a whisper. I just want him to open up to me.

There's a long pause, and I can actually feel Joseph's heart pounding against my hand still at his chest. "A lot of death. A lot of murder."

I bring a hand to my lips in horror. "I'm sorry," I say in a choked voice, feeling tears well up in my eyes.

"It's okay," he replies thickly. But I know it's not. He's fucking hurting, and it tears me up. "I'd just rather not talk about it." My eyes flicker down to my lap, then back to his. I want him to talk. I want him to open up to me.

I know how he feels, not wanting to talk about things. But it helped me, so much that I know for sure I wouldn't be the person I am without having someone to confide in. Even if it was just a counselor at school. It's good to talk it out.

"Please?" I plead with him.

He shakes his head, and the look in his eyes tells me not to push him. I nod, trying not to feel like he's pushing me away. My eyes focus on the closet, where the journal is. Maybe that's his way.

I glance over at the closet. "Can I read it?"

"The journal?" he asks, and I immediately nod my head. "You can read it any time you wish."

We sit together in silence, and I swear I can hear Joseph's heart beating in tandem with mine. After a moment I turn in his lap, looking him in the eyes. I see the pain in his dark gaze, and I hate that I've partly caused it by bringing up the subject. I just want to help make it go away.

"I'm sorry," I tell him, rubbing his arm.

He doesn't respond. Instead, he leans down and kisses me on the lips very gently. Emotions swell up from my stomach and I find myself wrapping my arms around his neck and pulling him into me, smashing my lips into his with fiery passion.

I feel him hesitate for a moment, but it only lasts for an instant. He wraps his arms around my waist and pulls me back into the bed.

I've never felt more connected to anyone in my life. The more I learn about Joseph, the more I want him.

The more I fall for him.

And that could be a very dangerous thing.

Joseph

ALTHOUGH HER HIPS *are steadied by the bench in front of her, the rope tying her wrists behind her back and hanging from the ceiling is what's keeping her upright. Her ankles are bound to the bench and spread for me. Her hips are tied down as well. She's dangling naked, completely at my mercy. With the blindfold on, she doesn't know where I am. Each time my feet smack on the floor, her fingers twitch slightly. Her shoulders are going to be hurting her soon. This has to come to an end soon enough. I pull back on the blow as I smack the riding crop against her ass one last time. She yelps as her upper body is swaying, although her lower body is tied so tightly she doesn't move from the waist down.*

Her ass is a beautiful shade of red. Some spots are a bit darker than the others. I trail the leather up the middle of her back; her body shivers, and her rose petal-colored nipples harden that much more. As I get to her arms and move forward, gently flicking the riding crop against her hard nipples, she moans.

It's only been thirty minutes, but she's so wet that her arousal is dripping down her thighs. I move the head of the riding crop up her neck and to her chin as I pull the blindfold off of her. The bright light startles her, and she sways away from me for just a moment as she closes her eyes. I allow it. Once she looks back at me, I bring my face closer to hers and plant a gentle kiss against her lips.

This is all because she got up from the table without asking for permission. Realistically, this isn't a punishment. I know she loved every minute of it. But that's what we're calling it.

"You do realize I own you," I tell her, my lips just an inch from hers. "You belong to me. Your freedom belongs to me." She holds my gaze as I speak to her. Her lips part in that beautiful way I've become addicted to.

She says her answer so sweetly, "Yes, Sir."

I walk around her, dropping the riding crop as I go and stroking my hard cock. I grip her hip in one hand although I don't need to, since she's not going anywhere.

I don't hold back when I fuck her.

And she takes it.

CHAPTER 20

Joseph

You can't keep telling me no.

I stare at the text message, nearly breaking the phone in my hand as I squeeze it, my anger rising and rising. I need to calm down. Every time this fuckface pisses me off, I fight with my flower. I'm not letting him come between us, and I don't give a damn what he wants.

I kept up my part of the bargain. I'm out.

They want the money back? They can come fucking get it.

I'm not dealing with their shit anymore. I pace the study, wanting to go back to the home I grew up in and beat the fucking piss out of him. But he never played fair. He'd pull a gun in a sword fight if he could. And he'd be damn proud of it. Going back there wouldn't be good.

The sound of Lilly turning off the water to the shower upstairs reminds me why I'm even letting him get to me. I finally have something worth giving a fuck about. This isn't the first or second or even the dozenth time I've had to put up with these assholes since I've left.

But lately I've been giving a fuck. I hear her pad across the bathroom upstairs. She's not a quiet little thing. Not in the least. The thought makes me smile until I hear the ping from my phone.

I scowl, looking down as my blood heats.

You don't have a choice.

Pissed. If I had less restraint, I'd hurl the fucking phone into the wall and scream out. Instead I calmly set it on the desk, staring at the phone and thinking of all the ways I'd love to kill him. I could have strangled him in his sleep. So many times I wanted to. I should have. Leaving that sick fuck alive was a mistake.

My desktop computer is still alive with light. With the sun setting and the thick curtains nearly closed shut, the study is dark. The faint glow of the computer draws me to it, back to the email Zander sent me.

If you'd like to chat, you can reach me here.
   -Z

It's the third time he's reached out to me.

He's yet to be straight with me, and I don't fucking trust him. I don't trust anyone.

My eyes dart to the ceiling as a thump followed by another thump tells me Lilly is up to something. I'm not sure what she's getting into, but I'm sure she'll be enjoying herself.

I have no one, I never have, but right now I need someone on my side. I need to protect Lilly. My fingers pick at my bottom lip. They itch for a glass of whiskey, to drown out the problems pestering me. The men behind the scenes of crime each reach out to me, each wanting me for something. But not with her here. I can't do that to her.

My phone pings again, and I don't even have to get up or even touch the phone to see the message.

Answer me!

I feel the grin grow on my face. He never did enjoy being ignored. Fucking prick can go fuck himself.

We had a deal, I take the fall and I get the fuck out of the *familia*. What happened to loyalty? I clench my teeth and bite back my anger, finally doing the sane thing and silencing the cell phone.

I toss my cell phone back onto the desk, rising from my seat and ignoring my past.

Zander, my *familia*... I can deal with them later. I leave the study, slamming the door shut behind me.

"Lilly!" I call out for my flower. For my beautiful distraction.

As I make it up the stairway, I see her scrambling out of her room. I've never called for her like this before. When she catches sight of my anger, she falls to the floor and into a perfect bow. A beautiful display of submission.

Her wet hair is sticking to her face and lying on the wooden floor of the hallway.

I climb up the last few steps and walk slowly to her, watching as her chest rises and falls. She thinks she's in trouble. My lips kick up into a smirk as she trembles slightly on the ground.

"What were you doing?" I ask her with a bit of humor in my voice.

She answers clearly and quickly, "I was trying to rearrange something." My brow furrows as I lower myself to the floor and cup her chin in my hand.

As I bring her lips up to mine, her body stays still, just as she should.

I plant a small kiss on her lips before searching her eyes. "Rearrange what?"

She swallows thickly. "I wanted to move the bed." I wait for more. At my silence, she adds, "So it would be across from the mirror." Her answer and the bright blush in her cheeks make me smile.

My flower. Ever the perfect distraction.

I rise, leaving her where she is and slowly taking off my worn leather belt. I let it slip through each loop on my pants slowly. "Did you ask permission?" I ask her. My voice is low and threatening. The punishment voice.

Her pupils dilate with lust as she shakes her head. "No, Sir."

I hold the belt in one hand, feeling my cock harden as I command her, "Get on all fours, now."

THE BELT CRACKS *against her skin again. "Ten!" Lilly cries out. Her hands are braced on the floor, her ass in the air. She's hanging over the edge of the bed, half on, half off. I run my hands down her trembling thighs and back up to her hot pussy. She's soaking wet for me.*

"You asked for this," I tell her, dropping the belt on her bed.

Lilly moans before answering, "Yes, sir." I've learned she needs this; she doesn't have many punishments anymore. What used to be a method of conditioning, a tool for her training, has now become the reward. And I'm more than happy to give it to her. I need it, too.

I brush my fingers along her folds, ready to pleasure her. But I stop when I see how red and swollen she is. I've been using her often, and my touch is rough. It's not surprising that she's sore.

As I run my fingers from her entrance to her clit, I wait for her to tell me, but she doesn't. Her forehead pinches, and she bites into her bottom lip. I do it again and she closes her eyes tight, but still she doesn't tell me I'm hurting her. It makes me angry. All this time, and she still doesn't talk to me. She wants me to open up to her, but she can't even tell me when I'm hurting her? I close my eyes and let out a frustrated sigh. She'll learn, I know she will. She's almost as stubborn as me, but I'll teach her.

"Get on all fours," I tell her as I unbutton my pants. I'm still waiting as I get behind her. Putting trust in the fact that she knows to tell me, and if nothing else she has a safe word. But she never utters it.

"You asked for a safe word, Lilly," I admonish her, placing my hand on her lower back. "But you're not even using it." She stills and looks back over her shoulder at me with frightened eyes. She realizes she's disappointed me. I leave her to grab the oil, and she gets up from her position, ready to protest, her soft voice apologizing.

She's breathing frantically until she sees the ointment in my hand.

This'll make her feel better.

"Did I tell you to move?" I asked her.

Lilly's quick to get back into position. "No, Sir," she breathes. The oil is cool on my fingers, so I warm it for a moment, massaging it between my hands before pressing my hand against her pussy. She winces for a moment, sucking a breath between her teeth.

I tell her as I massage her hot cunt, "I don't want to hurt you. If you desire pain, I'll give it to you in a way that's acceptable. But never like this." Her eyes close as I speak. She should know better. I don't want to injure her. I can give her what she craves in other ways.

"I'm sorry, Sir," she whispers her apology. "I just want to please you."

"You already do."

I move my fingers and spread the oil to her puckered hole, gently pressing my finger into her tight ring. My other hand is placed on her lower back as her mouth gapes from the sudden intrusion, and she nearly pushes away from me.

"Push back, my flower." Her back curves as she obeys me, my finger sliding farther in.

There's not an inch of her that I won't claim. But only when she's ready.

CHAPTER 21

Lilly

I LIE in my plush bed, staring up at the ceiling, my breasts gently rising and then falling with each breath. I can't stop thinking about Joseph. All the things he's gone through. The terrible life he's had.

I feel for him.

I wish I could be there for him. But he won't let me. I grab my blue pillow I brought from home and hug it against my chest.

I know why. He wants to appear strong, doesn't want me to think he's weak.

He needn't bother. I know he's strong, surviving what he's been through. I close my eyes and shake my head. He just needs to let me in.

I know he drinks when I lie down at night, trying to suppress those unwanted memories, smother those dark feel-ings. I saw him last night, drinking while writing in his journal. My heart hurt for him, seeing him sitting there vulnerable, and in pain. I stare at the journal, now laying on my bed.

I hate to see him when he's like that. Alone with his thoughts. Consumed by his past. He becomes a different man and puts me aside. I *loathe* it.

He needs someone to help him get over his past. And I want to be that person.

Isn't that what I'm supposed to do? Be there for him, like he's trying to be here for me?

I just want to get to know him. I don't like how he shuts me out, or when he goes to his study late at night. I'm grateful he lets me read what he's written. In a lot of ways that's his way of talking it through. Talking to me.

He needs that. I know firsthand how powerful it can be to just talk things out. Even if it's just your school guidance counselor. Maybe if I open up to him, he might then finally open up to me.

Gathering my courage, I sit up in bed and roll over onto the edge, my feet dangling off the side. I'm about to slip into a pair of plush white slippers, when I hear an angry shout downstairs. My heart racing, I slip off the bed and rush from the room.

As I'm rushing up the hallway to Joseph's study, the voices get louder. He's arguing about something with another man. Their voices are muffled, so I can't understand exactly what they're saying, but it doesn't take a genius to know whatever it is, it's not good.

Stay out of it, the voice in the back of my head warns. I know I shouldn't go there. My blood is freezing, and my heart refuses to beat because yells are coming from both Joseph and someone else. It's more than a heated argument. But my feet are moving before I can stop them. I have to see. I have to make sure he's okay.

But I can't go unarmed. The thought chills my spine, paralyzing my movements before sending me quickly on a different path.

I make it down the hall into Joseph's room, the voices rumbling like thunder throughout the house, making my blood freeze. I hear Joseph yell something that sounds like an awful threat. I've never heard him sound so angry. Fuck, I'm scared.

I rush into Joseph's closet, shaking and trembling, my heart skipping every other beat. The room spins around me as I steady my clammy palms on my thighs. I can hardly breathe. What the fuck did I get myself into?

He was in the mafia.

He was a bad man.

I take in an unsteady breath, staring at the suits that block the gun rack. I didn't for one second think he had anything to hide other than his dark past.

My fingers are trembling as I push his suits aside and swallow thickly at the sight of the guns. I stand there for a moment, my heart thump thump thumping as the noises downstairs gets louder. Staring at all the cold hard steel, my heart bounces around like a fighter in a cage.

I've used a gun before, but only for target practice. I don't know which to choose.

But I don't have time to sit here debating with myself. Joseph might need me. My throat closes as I quickly grab one of the Glocks and check if it's loaded. It is. The click of the gun makes my heart pound faster, but I rush out of the closet and out of his bedroom, and down the hall to his study, holding the gun down carefully at my side and trying to be quiet for once in my life.

I stop to the side of the door of his study, my heart racing, and dare to peek inside. My heart pounds. Thump. Thump.

Thump. The cold steel seems to heat as my palm sweats, making my grip on it weak.

Joseph's sitting at his desk, his face a mask of rage and there's a man in a black suit standing in the center of the room with his arms crossed across his chest.

They're arguing with each other, the man in black waving his hands sporadically before running his hand over his shiny bald head. Neither of them can see me from this angle, so I slip into the study, hiding behind the table, eavesdropping on their conversation. I can hardly keep my hands from trembling and the grip on the gun slips a little as I listen.

"The *familia* wants you back," the man is saying, his voice incredibly harsh. "Did you think they just forgot about you when you left?" He has a thick accent, but it sure as fuck isn't Italian. I'm trying to be quiet, but I feel like they're going to hear me just from my breathing.

"I don't give a fuck what they think," Joseph growls.

"Oh really? Do you really want to play this game?"

"I don't want to play anything. I'm done with that life. I'm a different man." The confidence in Joseph's voice makes me proud of him. I find myself nodding my head, although my heart is still begging me to get the fuck out of here.

The man in black lets out a harsh laugh. "You're not done until the *familia* says you're done." His quiet answer makes me want to peek around the table. My fingers grip the edge, but I can't do it. I'm frozen in place. "You can lie to yourself all you want, but it doesn't change the fact that you've killed in the name of the *familia*. That'll never go away, no matter how hard you try to forget, or no matter how many lies you try to tell yourself."

My heart stutters. *Joseph's killed people.* Goosebumps run over every inch of my skin.

There's a moment of silence, and I swear the only thing I can hear is the pounding of my heart. I'm afraid even Joseph and the man in black can hear it. Maybe that's why they're quiet; they know I'm in the room.

"You have ten seconds to get the fuck outta here," Joseph growls suddenly, his voice dark and deadly. My blood chills at the note in his voice. I don't think I've ever heard him so angry, so ruthless. It lets me know that whoever this man is, he's really gotten under Joseph's skin.

There's another pause, almost a hesitation, as if the man is wondering if he should press his luck and call Joseph's bluff. *Please don't.* My pointer finger steadies on the gun in my hand, although I'm too afraid to even open my eyes. I can barely hear the man respond, "The *familia* will be waiting for you."

He turns to leave, and when he does, I dare a peek from behind my hiding place. I catch a glimpse of dark hair, dark cold eyes and handsome features that remind me of Joseph's, except his are marred by the absolute ruthlessness stamped on his face.

For an instant, his cold eyes meet mine.

Fuck.

I sink down almost immediately, but I think he saw me. *I know he did.*

I can hear Joseph rise and follow the man out, the sounds of their shoes smacking against the ground so much softer than the sound of my wild heart. *He saw me. Fuck!!*

Before I can even move, Joseph returns and closes the door.

I sit there, clinging to the gun, my heart pounding, wondering what I should do. I'm fucking scared. I don't know what kind of shit Joseph is in, but I want no part in it. The man claimed Joseph killed before. He *killed* people.

After a moment, I decide to remain hidden until Joseph leaves the room, however long that takes.

But I don't get the chance.

"You can stop hiding now, flower," Joseph says, the sudden sound of his voice making my heart jump.

I close my eyes, swallowing thickly, and then slowly rise to my feet as a feeling of dread and two words run through my mind.

Oh fuck.

CHAPTER 22

Joseph

I CAN'T STAND the look in Lilly's eyes, accusing me. All this time she's been reading my journal, looking at me as though I'm a wounded animal. I don't want her sympathy. But her kindness and the sweet side she's given me have been addictive. I've grown to crave them.

Now she sees me for who I really am. What I represent, and where I came from. As if she didn't know. How did she think I got this fucked up?

You can't have one without the other.

"Hand me the gun," I command as I hold out my hand, and she's quick to look down at her hands as if only now realizing what she's holding. She rises slowly, her shoulders hunching in slightly and takes a step forward, handing it to me and quickly backs away. She looks around the room, still processing everything.

I gently set the gun on the table before turning back to her.

"What did you hear?" I ask her. More for her own safety than anything else. My brother isn't going to let up. I need to know what she heard.

She doesn't answer me. She stares at me wide-eyed with a mix of fear and something else.

I raise my voice and give her the command again, "What did you hear?" My heart hammers in my chest. I hate the look in her eyes. The way she's looking at me. I want my Lilly back. *My flower.*

"Nothing," she barely answers. Her voice is only just above a murmur. I narrow my eyes at her, hating that she's lying to me. I open my mouth to admonish her, but she cuts me off.

"I didn't sign up for this!" Lilly's voice wavers as she raises it. Her eyes are glazed with tears as her body trembles. Leaning forward, I can feel the anger radiating off of her in waves. As though I betrayed her.

"Who did you think I was Lilly?" I ask her, my head tilting and my voice low, filled with my own anger. She's a smart woman, she knew what she was signing up for. She had to know.

She stares at me with a look of contempt, but tears cloud her eyes. She shakes her head, unable to speak. She keeps looking at the door and then back at me. I can practically hear what she's thinking. She doesn't want me anymore. She doesn't want *this* anymore. I'm not the man in the books she reads. I'm not the poor boy whose memories of abuse are coming to front.

She thinks I'm *one of them*. One of the villains.

She swallows thickly and takes a step forward.

"Kneel," I give her the command, but she doesn't obey. She stares back at me, her eyes wide and disbelieving. My heart freezes. Don't deny me, Lilly. Don't do this. What we have is so good. It's so right.

"No," she says and shakes her head. "I want to leave!" she screams at me. My chest clenches with pain at the conviction in her voice. "The contract says that I can leave at any time." Her voice shakes as she speaks, mirroring the trembling of her body.

I can't let her go. I won't.

They've seen her. I saw the look in Ricky's eyes when he left.

They'd use her as a tool to get me. I take two steps closer to her, and she takes two away from me until her back hits the wall. She's staring back at me with her fists clenched, and her breathing is coming in sporadically. Her eyes flash with challenge, but they also contain fear. She's scared of me. It fucking kills me to see that look in her eyes.

I brace my palm on the wall beside her head, leaning forward and whispering into her ear, "You aren't going anywhere."

The only sound I can hear is her breathing. As though it contains her hate for me in this moment. She swallows thickly before answering, "You lied to me." The hurt in her voice is surprising. As if that's my biggest offense. Telling her she can go, and then taking it away.

I kiss her neck gently, but she's stiff and I wouldn't attempt to kiss on her lips at this moment. I pull away from her and rest my hand against her neck, my fingers wrapping around her throat in a possessive hold. "I've never lied to you Lilly," I speak softly, staring at her plump lips rather than the daggers in her eyes. "The game has changed though. You shouldn't have let him see you." I chance a look at her face, and her expression is one of sadness, her eyes staring at the hardwood floors.

Again she swallows, quiet and no longer fighting me. But

that's only because she doesn't know how to fight back yet. She will, I know she will. She has too much fight in her to give up so easily.

"You directly disobeyed me," I say quietly; that draws her attention to me, and the sadness is once again replaced by anger. I prefer that. Because at least with anger, there's passion. I crave her passion.

"You need to go to your cage now." I deliver the blow.

Her lips part, and I can practically hear the words on her tongue, *"Yes, Sir."* But instead she snaps her lips shut, looking me straight in the eyes and refusing to obey yet again. It makes me want to smile. Her defiance, her new game move. I'll take it; I'll take anything she's willing to give me.

We're both quiet as I lead her to her room. I silently open the cage, and she gets in without a fight. That's not to say she doesn't have one. I can feel her disobedience rolling off of her in waves. I shut the door just as I did before, not locking it. I never have, and I never will.

She stares at me through the bars of the cage, with a look of pure hate shining back.

But she doesn't use her safe word, and I cling to that knowledge.

CHAPTER 23

Lilly

I LIE IN MY BED, naked, the cool air from the ventilation system caressing my bare skin. I'm counting the days until this is all over. Just thinking that hurts my heart, my hand moving to it and tears pricking my eyes.

It hurts to think Joseph maybe isn't the man I thought he was. I knew he was hiding dark secrets, but this is just too dark for me. He won't let me leave. But as soon as he deals with this mess, as he says, then I'm gone. Money or no money, contract or not. I don't care.

It'll all be over. I roll over onto my side, clinging to the small blue pillow I brought with me from home and ignoring the pain in my chest.

At the same time, I don't want it to end. It's crazy. I both hate it and love it. Hate *him* and love *him*.

I blow out a frustrated breath as I think about my predicament, think about the position I'm in.

It makes me want to fight him, knowing he's keeping me here. And I'm getting addicted to it.

But even with the urge to be belligerent, I still obey him. Only to a degree. Pushing my limits, testing him. He knows it too, and that only makes me push harder. Because I want him to push me harder. The knowledge makes me lower my eyes to the beautiful white comforter.

And I still have feelings for him, even with my doubts. I can't deny how strong they are. How could I not?

A part of me hates myself for feeling that way. But I can't help it. I can't snap my fingers and erase what I feel just because Joseph may have done some horrible things. We have a connection, something that I've never had with anyone, though it feels very strained right now. Because of me. Because his past won't leave him alone.

I stretch out my leg, and lay it over the outfit he has laid out for me. My eyes are drawn to the beautiful short dress. Don't know why he laid it out. It's not like I'll be wearing it.

He wants to tempt me to wear it, that voice at the back of my head says. *So he can have a reason to punish me when I don't.*

As if he needs a reason. He can do whatever he wants to me.

He owns me.

I can't even lock my bedroom door.

I never have a moment of privacy.

That's the part my romance novels left out. The cold, harsh reality of never having a moment to yourself, never being able to do anything without approval. It was fun and games before, when I wasn't angry at him. When I wanted it as much as he did. But it changed.

I hate that I even have to ask to work on my novel. But it's not like he denies me that privilege. He always gives permission when I ask. Somehow, that makes it more infuriating.

I wish I could be more pleased with him. Instead, I feel like I'm a spoiled pet throwing a tantrum.

I'm so confused.

My thoughts are swept away as I hear the soft creak of the bedroom door.

I hear him walk into the room, but I only move my head just enough to peek at him. My breath catches at the sight. He looks handsome as usual, dressed in black dress pants and a white dress shirt opened at the chest. I don't get off the bed to kneel or greet him. That's why I know I won't be wearing those clothes. I'm done playing. He can just throw me in the damn cage until he lets me go.

His eyes find my naked body and I blush fiercely, though I don't know why. It's nothing he hasn't seen before. Looking at him, I'm feeling so many emotions that I have to turn away, my chest heaving.

Anger. Hurt. Betrayal. Lust.

They're all there.

I startle slightly as I feel his arms encircle my waist. His hot lips find my neck and I find myself leaning back into him, my lips parting in a soft sigh, my nipples pebbling. I've missed his touch. My eyes close; he feels so good. My arm wraps around his, betraying me, but I don't care. I just want to feel him for a moment. Just a moment.

"I know you're still angry with me, Lilly," he says softly in my hair, his breath hot on my neck. I can feel his big, hard cock pressing against my ass, and I desperately want him inside of me. *Make love to me. Make me forget. Please, make me forget.*

I wish he couldn't read me so well. And I don't want to really respond. But I know he's expecting an answer.

"Yes, Sir," I say softly, my words sounding a bit stiff. I've come to hate them. But I love saying them at the same time. I'm just one big walking contradiction.

He runs his hand down my stomach, and circles it around my pubic hair. "When you shower, make sure you shave."

Anger swells up my throat, and I swallow. I'm glad he can't see me roll my eyes. He knows I'll shave; I just haven't gotten a chance to take a shower yet. I think he just knows that I'm pissed and wants to make me even angrier. He wants to rule over me. Fuck him!

"You're an asshole!" The words spew from my lips before I can stop them.

His arms leave my waist. I'm relieved and miss his touch all at the same time. I fucking hate how he makes me feel. "Why are you angry with me?" he asks, his voice even and low. Deadly.

I turn to face him, no longer able to hide the anger I feel. "You lied to me."

Joseph clenches his jaw. "I already told you that I didn't."

"And I'm supposed to believe that? That man said you killed people. How do you explain that?"

"Lilly, I'm going to ask you not to talk about that. It has nothing to do with us."

My jaw nearly drops as I stare at him with wide eyes. "Nothing to do?" I ask breathlessly, stabbing my finger into the mattress. "I'm a fucking Slave to a murderer! That's what I am! How do you think that makes me feel?"

Anger flashes in his eyes. I've really pissed him off by calling him a murderer.

He stares at me for a long moment, his chest heaving, the veins standing out on his neck. For a second, I think he'll even strike me. Maybe I just want him to, so I can have a real reason to hate him or at least a reason not to love him. But his next words make my blood run cold.

"Go to your cage."

I open my mouth to protest, but I snap it shut. It's useless. This is what I wanted anyway.

Tears well up in my eyes, but I fight them back. I don't know why I said anything. I should've known what would happen. All I needed to do was to shut the fuck up and keep counting the days until this was over.

I turn around, drop to my knees, and crawl inside my cage, hating him every second of the way.

He shuts the cage door before I'm even in the back of it. But he doesn't lock it. He never does. I wish he would. My heart breaks as I hold back the sob.

I glare at him balefully from in between the bars. He looks down at me with both pity and anger in his eyes. For some reason, it pisses me the fuck off, yet again.

"I'll spend every fucking day here in this cage if it means I can get away from you," I snarl with venom. I don't know why I say the words. I know I don't even mean it. But I can't help myself.

I regret it the moment I say it though.

I wait for him to say something nasty in response, but he doesn't. His face is an impassive mask, but his eyes are a storm of emotion. I've hurt him with my words, I can feel it. It hurts me to know that. I really shouldn't have done that. God, I'm such a bitch. Looking at the swirl of emotion in his dark eyes makes me hate myself.

He was opening up to me, and now he'll be closed off.

Fuck, I'm sorry. *I'm so fucking sorry.*

But I can't bring myself to say anything. My throat's closed off, and the tears roll down my cheeks.

I don't know why.

After a moment, his eyes heavy, Joseph turns and walks from the room, leaving me alone in my cage.

A feeling of guilt washes over me as soon as he's gone, along with a wave of loneliness and I can't stop the tears that are suddenly falling freely down my face.

I really should be careful what I wish for.

Joseph

HER NAILS dig into my forearms, scratching down my arms and leaving marks as I fuck her ruthlessly, claiming her once again. "Keep fighting me, my flower," I tell her as my hips buck into her and the bed shakes beneath us.

It's been three days since I've been able to feel the warmth of her cunt wrapped around my dick. Not that she hasn't wanted me, since her anger seems to only intensify her desire. I stare into her eyes, and she stares back at me with the same fierceness. In this moment I don't know who owns who.

She so close, I can see it on her face, but she's yet to ask permission.

"Are you trying to cum before I allow you to?" I pull away from her, pulling out of her warmth and leaving her on the edge of her release. I would have gladly given it to her, had only she asked. She breathes heavily, her blue eyes swirling with defiance.

The room fills with the sounds of our heavy breathing.

Hate fuck. Makeup sex. I'm not sure what this is, but I'm hopeful that once it's over, she'll forgive me. I want her to look at me the way she used to.

I crawl up her body, my hard dick wet with her arousal, pressing into her hip. Her expression softens as I gentle my hands at her hip. She doesn't know what to think as I kiss up between her breasts along her collarbone and up her neck.

"You only need to ask me," I say and stare at her lips, wishing I could kiss her like I used to. My eyes dart to hers, and I feel this familiarity of what used to be between us. I take a chance, pressing my lips to hers.

She kisses me back before breaking the kiss and asking, "Please, Sir." There's hesitation in her voice before she adds, "I miss you."

There's no trace of anger on her face. Only sadness. I'm not sure if this will last. But at least I have my flower for a moment.

CHAPTER 24

Joseph

THE MARKS in the journal are smooth as the pen glides against the paper. The pages are worn and old at this point, and nearly come to the end. It's fitting, seeing as how I've come to the final scene between myself and my father.

The Romanos were easy to gun down. They didn't even see it coming. My father took the entire crew. Eighteen men. The first four littered the front of the restaurant with bullets. I remember how the glass broke, shattering onto the ground in splintered pieces. I stood in the background, my father to my right, my brother to my left. The screams and gunshots rang out clearly. Blood flooded the streets that night on both sides, although heavy in the Romanos. Their wives were with them. Their children were with them. Their deaths were quick. With a gun in each hand I walked up with my father, the glass crunching beneath my boots.

I shot a bullet in each of their heads from my guns. Evidence. I continued shooting until they were both empty. Part of me hoped that my father was going to put a bullet in the back of my head. Every bullet that went off, I expected it. I was meant to take the fall. And I didn't think that required me being alive at the end of this.

My father gave me a look with a hint of fear when he told me not to mention a single name. I already knew not to. What's more memorable than seeing fear for the first time in my father's eyes, was the cold look of my brother's face. I saw jealousy there. My father was willing to trust me with this task. A son who he knew never loved him. And my brother hated me for it.

Even if I was going to go away for life. He didn't like that I got any approval from our father, or any respect from the men of the familia. *But I didn't agree to do it for either of those reasons.*

I never uttered a word. I was ready to take the blame and get the death penalty or go to prison for life; I didn't care which. I deserved to be punished for my sins. All of them. But the cops let me go. They followed me, they waited. They were pissed I wouldn't talk, and they anticipated that letting me out would send up red flags to everyone on the streets.

They thought my *familia* would come for me. They thought the target they put on my back would have me running back to talk and give them the information they wanted in exchange for protection.

Their error was thinking that I gave a damn. I was ready to die. I didn't care how. It didn't matter to me who pulled the bullet.

My father didn't make a move. If anything, he knew I was honest, and he gave me the only thing I truly wanted. Freedom from his rule. But now that my brother is gearing up to take over, my past is coming back to haunt me.

I'm not going back. I don't care how many men my brother sends here. I'll kill them all before I go back. I just hope it doesn't come to that. I haven't pulled a trigger in a long fucking time. But I sure as fuck haven't forgotten how to do it.

The pen stills on the paper as I hear the faint padding of Lilly's bare feet against the floors behind me. Her anger has waned tremendously. She's not trying to fight me like she was before.

Maybe she's forgiven me. Maybe she's realized that she wasn't as angry as she thought she was. She was hurt because she thought she knew me.

In many ways she does though, more than anyone else ever has.

Or maybe it's because I stopped fighting her.

I've been going easy on her. I don't want to give her a reason to go back to that cage. I don't want to give her a reason to fight me any more than she already has. I don't see a way out of this, other than meeting with my brother. But to do that, I have to leave Lilly, and not something I can't risk. I *won't* risk her.

"Joseph?" she asks me.

Although she's used my real name, she still kneels beside the chair. I never know which side of her I'm going to get until she approaches me. It's a funny thing. I thought I didn't want a Submissive. I didn't want someone else to control what we do, and when and what our rules are. But Lilly's gotten under my skin. I'm bending for my flower. I'd rather do that than see her wilt.

"Yes?" I turn to her, petting her hair and waiting for her to look up at me.

She visibly swallows and clasps her hands in her lap. She seems nervous, which in turn makes me nervous, but of course I don't show her that. I'm her Master at all times, and I must be strong for her.

"What are you doing?" she asks, her eyes on the journal.

I pat my lap and say, "Come sit with me." She stands

slowly and obeys me, but there's still hesitation in her actions. I've yet to earn her trust back. Even if she gives me these small moments, I know what we once had is broken.

I place my journal on her lap. My heart races in my chest, every bit of vulnerability I've ever had is documented within. I don't know why I write it all down. Maybe the dark scenes that haunt me late at night will leave me if only I write them down.

"I like to write things I remember." Her pale blue eyes focus on mine through her thick lashes. And then look back down to the journal. I can see those wheels turning in her head; she wants to ask more. I don't wait. I pull her closer to me, my fingers tickling the curve of her waist as I sit back in the chair. "I used to do very bad things, Lilly." My heart pounds in my chest as I confess to her, "I've written down some more for you." I swallow thickly. "These ones are just for you." My body chills at the thought of her hating me when she reads them. It's all the truth of what I've done. I can't forgive myself, but maybe she will. She's kinder than me. She met me when I'd tried to move on.

Her breathing comes in a little louder. She licks her lips slightly and then asks, "Why did you do them?" The hurt in her voice kills me.

"You didn't want me to turn out to be a bad man, did you?" She wants there to be good in all people. I can tell that about her. It's one of the qualities I find endearing about her. I think that's one of the reasons she's so angry with me. I disappointed her. But I swear I tried.

Her voice cracks as she answers, "You aren't a bad man." She can't even look me in the eyes as she says it. She knows she's lying, and it breaks my heart.

"I didn't have much of a choice." I know I had one, but it was kill or be killed. For the first time in a long time, she lays

185

gently against my chest. Her small hand rubs circles over my heart. I miss her comforting touch.

"Would you like to read it?" The offer spills from my lips in an attempt to tell her what I had been through and explain without having to actually tell her. I don't want to recount it all over again. I put it into this journal so I can forget. But maybe if she knows everything, the explanation of how I left and why, she can forgive me.

She doesn't hesitate to nod, the word slipping between her lips, "Yes." The eagerness in her response makes me smile.

"This is different from what I thought it would be," she says softly. The way she speaks makes it seem as though what she's telling me is a secret.

"It is for me, too." I have to agree; this isn't at all what I had in mind when I first laid eyes on Lilly.

I wasn't lying when I said the game's changed.

"How is it different for you?" she asks, playing at the hem of her dress. I suppose I'll have to go first before she'll tell me what she was thinking.

"That the Master/slave relationship is only for short spurts. I'm not stupid, Lilly. I don't control you. But I don't want to, either." I want something different from her now. More than just acceptance as her Master. More than forgiveness. Although I'm not sure what, exactly.

She looks a little bit upset and hesitant. I wish she'd just forgive me. I want to put her at ease. That's all I've been trying to do for the past week.

"I'm sorry, I've been…" Lilly's voice trails off. "I knew you… I knew you had…" She looks away, unable to finish.

"It's in my past. I promise you." I just need her to believe it. I know she doesn't want to fight me anymore. "I'm not the man I once was." She must know it's true. She knows me better than anyone ever has.

Her nod is small, but accepting. I can see it in her eyes that she believes me.

"Where does that leave us? Both of us thinking this was something it's not… and you… figuring," she waves her hand in the air, shifting in my lap.

I cup her small chin in my hand, tilting those soft lips closer to mine as I say, "It just means that sometimes we'll play, and sometimes we'll just be us."

She looks up at me and asks, "And what is that?"

I don't know how to answer her, so I'm quiet.

"Even if we aren't playing, you still need to treat me as though I'm your Master." Although it's a statement, it feels as though I'm asking her a question. I feel wrong for telling her that since all this time we've nearly been playing scenes. But I know what she's about to read. And I don't want her to think any differently of me. I am her Master, and it should stay that way. Regardless of what she reads. Regardless of how well she gets to know me.

"Yes, Sir."

"HOLD STILL, MY FLOWER," I tell Lilly as her back rests against the wall. "Hands at your side," I say as I push her palms against her thighs. She's naked before me, finally obeying me again. It feels as though we're playing house. Like this is all pretend. We're ignoring what lies beyond these walls. My familia, *the fact that she can't leave. Pretending to be blind to what's meant to keep us apart.*

I get on my hands and knees, putting my face between her thighs and inhaling her sweet scent. Judging by her gasp, she didn't expect it. I smile against her heat before taking a languid lick and pulling back to look her in the eyes.

"Ride my face, Lilly," I tell her, noting how her eyes widen as

she comprehends my words. "Take your pleasure from me. Cum freely."

I place my hands on the inside of her knees, allowing her legs to bend slightly. She rocks helplessly into my face, hesitant at first. But as I groan with approval, her hips grind harder and soft moans spill from her lips.

So long as she obeys me, I'll give her everything she wants. Every pleasure, every need. I just need her to obey me. I need her to stay with me.

CHAPTER 25

Lilly

I TAKE A DEEP BREATH, my fingers trailing over the high quality leather of Joseph's journal. I'm partway through reading it. I don't know if I'm ready today for more of the bad things that I know I'll find out while reading it, but I'm going to go through with it anyway. I want to see what happened in his life. It makes me feel that much more connected to him.

A ray of sunshine hits the golden latch of the journal, reflecting a flash into my eyes.

I'm curled up in Joseph's sunroom, reclined in a white, plush fabric recliner, soaking in the warmth of the sun. The view from here is gorgeous. The sky is a clear azure blue, and the ground is covered with a thick layer of white snow that reflects the sunlight, filling the room with brightness.

It's lifting my mood. I'm already feeling better from these past few days with the new rules Joseph has set for us. I like the idea he had about playing scenes. And I love that he's opening up to me bit by bit. He's adding details and writing notes to benefit my understanding of what happened. He won't talk to me about it though; the journal is all I get. He won't even be in the same room when I read it. Even now, he's in the kitchen because he knows I'm reading it.

I open the journal to the last passage I stopped on and pick up where I left off. It doesn't take long before I'm deeply engrossed in his story. Now that I know how the story ends, everything he's written is so clear. But when I reach a passage that's so heartbreaking, about his mother, I can't keep the tears from falling from my eyes.

"This is hard," I say thickly, wiping the tears from my cheek with the back of my hand.

I have to close the book. I can't read any more right now. I just can't believe all the things that Joseph has gone through. I feel absolutely awful for him.

I haven't forgotten that he's keeping me here. That I'm a prisoner. But I wouldn't leave if he told me to. If he commanded me. I'd refuse.

As soon as I see him, I'm going to crawl in his lap and kiss him and try to give him all the comfort that I'm capable of giving. I know he doesn't like to be held and he doesn't like sympathy, but I need it as much as he does.

But for now, I'll keep playing our game and pretend like I don't know that he's avoiding me because I'm reading the journal. He'll pretend he doesn't know that it kills me to see what he's been through. I don't mind playing this game, because it only makes me closer to him.

I push the journal onto the ottoman and grab my laptop, wiping under my eyes and my nose as I move.

I need to relieve some serious stress. I sniffle again, opening up the laptop as I sag in the seat. Right fucking now. And there's nothing that helps me to relieve it more than writing. It's always been my therapy for when my emotions are heightened, or I'm feeling down. It's the perfect way to release my emotions. Joseph needs something like that. I told him that.

And he told me that's what I am to him. My heart hurts, remembering his words.

I open on my laptop screen, my mind overflowing with ideas to use for the story. It should be easy. I have so much material to work with. So many emotions to play off of.

I'm about to turn over to the Word document screen, when an email notification pops up on my screen.

From: Aida White
  To: Lilly Wade
  Subject: MY BABY IS GONE
  Lilly

My hands are shaking as I type these words. I don't know who to talk to, but I need to talk to someone. I haven't stopped crying since this morning. My baby is gone. I can't believe it. How I wish I would have turned my life around sooner. If only he would've waited just a little while longer and mommy would have been there for him. I feel like such a worthless piece of shit. I bet that's what you think of me. And you're not wrong.

The police called me this morning to tell me that Zach got into a fight. He was stabbed to death. He died this morning.

I know you were someone that was important to him, they gave me your email. You have to be someone special because he would talk about you when he called me. I just want to thank you for being there for my baby when I couldn't.

Sincerely,

Zach's mom, Aida

I stare at the screen in disbelief, my stomach twisting in agony. I don't believe it. It can't be true. This has to be some sick cruel joke. I shake my head. This didn't happen. This woman is a liar. She's a liar!

I shake my head, pushing the laptop away, refusing to believe Zach is dead.

It might be one of his friends playing a joke on me. I can't accept this. It has to be! Tears roll down my cheeks as I rise out of the chair. Not Zach.

I refuse to believe it.

He was going to get his life together. Even the parole officer said it. Things were going to be better for him.

"It's not true," I say over and over in denial. "This is a bunch of bullshit!"

I have to believe it's not true, but a growing fear grips my heart. I have to find out.

I jump up from my seat and rush through the house in search of a landline phone. I find one in Joseph's study. My hands fumble over the ancient thing while I nearly rip the phone out of the wall in my haste to pick up the receiver.

I quickly dial the parole officer's number. I know it by heart. Pick up. Pick up! My fingers twist around the cord as I pace the small area.

It rings three times before someone answers.

"Hello?" a woman's husky voice answers.

My lips are suddenly dry, and my words stick in my throat. *It's okay,* I tell myself. *You'll see. It was all a lie. He's okay*

I suck in a deep breath and then blurt, "It's Lilly Wade... I'm calling to... find out about... Zach White?" That's all I can manage.

I don't know if it's protocol to just say a name when calling to ask for information, but I can't say anything else. My throat feels so tight, I almost can't breathe.

The woman on the other end of the line gets it though, because I hear the tapping of keys.

Her next words nearly knock me off my feet.

"I'm sorry, Ms. Wade. He passed away this morning."

The phone slips from my fingertips and swings up against Joseph's desk with a bang. But I no longer care. The room is spinning around me. My heart is racing. I can't fucking think. Not him. I couldn't help him. But they were going to. They were going to save him. He told me they would. He told me he'd be fine!

Somewhere in the background, I hear the woman's voice coming out of the receiver, "Ma'am, are you there?"

I sink to my knees beside the desk, wrapping my arms around my chest, and begin rocking back and forth. Trying to calm myself. Trying to remember the moves I learned in yoga class to help me relax. But instead my rocking is fast. Too fast.

I'm not okay. It's not okay.

"No, no, no, no!" I repeat over and over, the tears rolling from my eyes, so hot my eyes are burning. I can't believe it. I failed him. I should have done more to help him. I should have snatched his ass and forced him in the car that day I saw him walk away from me.

It's all my fucking fault.

"Ma'am, are you all right?"

She tries again to get my attention several more times before hanging up, the sound of the dial tone mixing in with my quiet cries.

I don't even hear the sound of footsteps, but I'm suddenly pulled up into a hard chest by strong arms.

"What happened?" Joseph asks, pushing my hair out of my face as I try to calm down.

I can't answer him right away, the tears and sobs coming in even harder, seemingly brought on by his caring touch. But he waits patiently for me to get a hold of myself, his normally dark eyes filled with concern.

"Zach died," I sob when I can finally say the words. "He was murdered." Speaking haltingly, I tell him all about my relationship with the troubled kids in school and how I devoted a lot of myself to helping them and how special Zach was to me.

"I thought he was going to be okay." It's all I can say toward the end. His strong hand rubs my back in large, soothing circles.

Joseph frowns, squeezing me gently. "I'm so sorry. But this wasn't your fault, do you understand? You couldn't have changed what happened to Zach. No one could." I shake my head in denial before burying my face into his hard chest.

I want to scream at him, 'That doesn't make it right!', but when I pull away from him and look at the softness in his eyes, I know that he's only trying to make me see the truth. I couldn't save him, just like I couldn't save my mother. Just like my father couldn't save her. "Lilly, you can't save people from themselves. I know that. So much better than most people. But you try. And you never stop. You're a good person. Even if he's gone." I let out a small sob and try to pull away, but Joseph holds my chin firmly in his grasp and continues, "Even if he's gone, you can still help others. I'm sure you have. Even if you don't know it." He grips my chin and forces me to look into his eyes. The intensity that he gazes at me with actually stops my sobs and dries my tears. "I know you have."

I feel like shit. My heart is hurting. But I can't deny the

power he has over me. I shake my head, not fully believing him.

His next words steal the air from my lungs. "You've helped me." He loosens his grip on me to brush the hair from my face as he says softly, "More than you'll ever know.

I stare up into his eyes, and I see something I've never seen before, something so powerful it makes me weak in the knees. Something I'm not sure that I'm seeing because it's truly there, or because I want it to be there.

That must be it. I'm only imagining the love I see reflected in his eyes.

CHAPTER 26

Joseph

I THOUGHT it was her that was playing a game when we started this. But it's more clear to me now that I was the one playing. The bottle of whiskey is empty. I keep bringing it to my lips, forgetting that it's gone, having nothing to take this pain away.

There's life beyond the hollow shell I've been living in. There's a reason to fight, there's a reason to *feel*. Lilly's shown me that. My heart hurts for her. I wish I could give her something to take the pain away. But nothing can soothe grief. I know that all too well.

Over the last few days, she hasn't been herself. I told her she's blaming herself for something she couldn't control. It's something no one could have controlled. But she doesn't want to believe that.

I'll show her with time. I'll help her however I can. I just want her to be happy again.

Knock. Knock. Two soft knocks from the front entry distract me from my thoughts.

I've ordered her a new laptop. I put the bottle down on the end table and quickly make my way to the door. I'm eager to get her something that will make her smile. She's been burying herself in her writing. I'm hoping this will make her happy. Even if it's only for a moment.

When I open the door without checking, my heart stops. I hate myself this very second. I should have known better. Fool! I'm a fucking fool for letting my guard down.

I stare down the barrel of two guns, held by men I don't recognize, but I know who sent them. I stand there numb on the surface, but internally I'm screaming. How could I be so fucking stupid? I don't have a gun. I have nothing! And Lilly's upstairs. Vulnerable. It's my fault.

"What do you want?" I ask without giving in to the fear and reflecting it in my voice. My hand grips the door keeping me upright, as though without it, I'd fall.

Lilly. She's all I can think about. I start to walk outside, my hand closing the door behind me, but they step forward, crowding my space. I need to get them away from here. As far away from Lilly as I can.

"We can discuss this somewhere else," I say easily, as they ignore me and continue walking forward, pushing me back into my foyer. One closes the front door and locks it. I start thinking about where every gun I have in this house is located. I have them stashed away in every room. My eyes dart to the corner of the foyer; the one here is behind these two assholes, so I won't be able to get to the gun in the closet. There are two in the living room though. I only need to get these assholes to follow me in there. But that's closer to Lilly. Fuck! I try not to clench my jaw and ball my hands into fists at the thought.

I'm not sure if these men know she's here. I can't risk

them finding out. I wish I could tell her to run. To hide. I wish I could go back in time and never speak to her, never corrupt her with the sins of my past.

If only I could. I'd give it all up to keep her safe.

"You know how this ends, Joe," the one man says to my left. He's nearly bald and short, and his leather jacket is slightly too big for him. The man on his right is much taller, his military cut giving him an edge over the other fuckface. Both of them are holding their guns loosely. They're both arrogant. They think they've won. I take in a deep breath, quickly coming up with a plan. Something. Anything to keep her from them.

The bald man continues to point his gun at me as the other man asks, "We just need the code for your safe." I huff a grunt. Of course. Money. It's always about the money.

"And why would I tell you that?" I ask with a grin that doesn't reflect a single thing I'm feeling.

"Because if you do, we won't make you watch what we're gonna do to your girl." He smiles a crooked grin, showing his yellowed teeth. "We'll put you out of your misery first." The bald man's answer chills my blood. My heart pounds in my chest.

As I swallow thickly, registering what they're saying and trying not to give into the urge to beat the piss out of him, I see movement over the tall man's right shoulder.

Lilly.

I swear my heart stops. What the fuck is she doing?

"You need to go back where you came from," I tell the man standing in front of me, but I'm not speaking to him. I wish I could look at her as I talk, but I can't. I'm afraid they'll follow my line of sight, turn around and see her.

I'm fucking pissed as I say the same words louder. Both men seem thrown off by the command in my voice, but I don't care. I can't even think about them. She needs to listen. She needs to get out of here.

I dare to take a step forward when the floor creaks with Lilly's steps, it distracts them enough that they don't hear her; both men point their guns at my head. "You should go hide," I tell them, a sick grin on my face with false confidence in my voice. *Run, Lilly!*

Lilly must know that I'm speaking to her, but she doesn't listen. Of all the times I need her to just listen to me, now is the time. But she doesn't, she just continues forward, entering the foyer and holding a gun in her hands high, pointing at the tall man to my right.

"You have two minutes, Joe," the bald man says. "Or else Nicky here..." he sticks his thumb out pointing to the other man and turns his head slightly to look at him. My heart jumps up my throat when he does, because as he turns to look at his partner, he catches sight of Lilly. I see it all happen in slow motion.

Fuck!

He shouts and raises his gun at her, whipping around on his heels and I react instantaneously, pushing forward with all of my weight, shoving him down to the ground. All the sounds and screams turn to white noise, my lungs freezing, my heart beating frantically. A rush of heat takes over my body, nearly numbing me. I've never felt so much fear in my life.

"Run!" I yell at Lilly as several gunshots go off at once. Bang! Bang! Bang!

Lilly, not Lilly. My throat hurts from my screams as I fight for the gun. Trying to keep him from shooting it, but trying to look at Lilly. Run! Just run!

I hear her shrill scream as another bullet echoes off the wall. A stray piece of drywall falls into pieces and lands on the bald man's face. And then another gunshot, this one from the gun I'm fighting over. The jolt of the trigger being pulled loosens the grip this fucker has on it.

The bullet flies through the air and strikes me in my upper forearm. Fuck! I curse under my breath. In and out in the blink of an eye. I feel the urge to reach up and grab the wound, but I can't. I won't let it stop me from strengthening my hold on the gun. Nothing will stop me.

"Lilly!" I call for her. I can't hear her. "Lilly!"

My fingertips slip against the gun as the bastard kicks me in the gut. Both of us are wrestling on the ground, trying to rip the gun out from each other's grip. The pain from the shot in my arm shoots up and down my shoulder. I ignore it, merely clenching my teeth from the screaming pain as I continue to fight.

His head is close to the thick front leg of the foyer table. I could take a risk and stop fighting for the gun, going for his chin instead and try to slam his head into the hardwood. But that would mean letting go of the gun that I almost have a grip on. His fingertips fumble at the trigger again, a bullet whizzing through the air and landing into the plaster wall. He flinches from the sudden shot.

I take advantage of the moment, hurling my body upward. Using my forearm instead of my hand, I smash the back of his head against the leg of the table. It doesn't do any real damage, but it makes him close his eyes. I'm able to jump forward and sink my teeth into his forearm and grab the gun the second he loosens his grip on it. In a swift moment, the gun is in my hands and I don't hesitate to put a bullet through his skull. *Bang!*

My heart races as I quickly raise the gun in my hands and prepare to shoot the other bastard. But instead I find Lilly, staring at the man lying still on the floor. Three gunshot wounds are visible from the blood staining his shirt.

Lilly doesn't look at me when I call her name, still gripping the gun in both of her hands. She's shaking.

I stand slowly with my hands up, looking between the two men dead on the floor. There's blood spilling from their open wounds and pooling on the marble floor beside them. At least it happened out here, where I can easily clean up this mess.

I can hardly look at Lilly. I'm full of shame. It's because of me that she had to fight for her life. I couldn't protect her. I brought this pain to her. It's my fault.

She drops the gun to the ground, and it hits the marble hard with a loud thud as she collapses into my open arms. The moment I close my arms around her, she sobs into my chest, trembling uncontrollably. As if my touch broke the trance.

I've put up with my brother and father for years. But they brought Lilly into this, and that firms my resolve.

I kiss Lilly's hair softly, rubbing soothing circles on her back. But I stare straight ahead at the blank wall, knowing I need to kill them. Tonight.

CHAPTER 27

Lilly

I'M a ball of nerves as I sit in Madam Lynn's office, my mind on what just happened.

I killed a man.

I still can't believe it. It's nearly impossible for me to process. I keep thinking that I'm going to wake up and find out this was all some horrible nightmare. I pull my legs up into the chair, wrapping my arms tightly around my knees.

But it's too fucking real.

Never in a million years would I have thought I'd wind up in a situation like this. It's like a real life action movie. Hell, it's even like one of my romance novels. Except there might not be a happy ending for this one.

The thought chills my blood.

Even worse, I thought Joseph was going to die. I saw him die. I know I did. I couldn't pull the trigger as the man came after me. But I saw Joseph. I saw the bullet.

My chest tightens as I remember the gun pointed at his head. God, I can hardly breathe remembering it. My heart felt like it was ripped from my chest. Even now I get cold sweats thinking about it. He was so close to death.

Had I not walked in right at that moment, he would've died. They were going to kill him.

I'm glad I shot that asshole. I'm glad he's dead. I'll never tell a soul. But I don't regret it. Not for a single moment.

And now I'm here. Stranded in an office in Club X. Joseph left me here, shoving cash into my purse and telling me that they'd protect me.

He pushed me away. He told me they would protect me, literally pushing me into the arms of people I don't even know.

And now I'm ready to leave. I rest my face on my knees. My eyes feel hot against my cool skin. I just want to get the fuck out.

I'm tired of being in this office. I either want to be with him, or I want to go home.

I'm tired of being a prisoner.

I know after what happened, he's pushing me away for my safety, trying to figure things out. And he wants me to be where he thinks I'm safe. I understand, I do. But I still don't want to be here. I feel helpless just sitting here and waiting around for I don't know how long.

I look around the office. It's so depressing. Just a medium-size room with a large oak desk littered with papers and not a single window.

Besides the lamplight, it's dark in here. Madam Lynn has been very nice to me and has done her best to make me feel comfortable with what she has to work with, but she hasn't come back in, I glance at the clock above the door, for almost two hours. I haven't seen *anyone* for hours. My heart flickers in my chest. I don't even know if Joseph is still here. I cover my face with my hand.

How could he just leave me here?

I shake my head and put my feet back on the ground. He has to know by now I can't live without him. Isn't it obvious that I love him? He must know.

Restless, I get up from my seat and pace the floor, wondering what the hell I should do. I want to leave, but I'm not sure if I'll be safe. And he told me to stay here. He practically pleaded with me to do as I was told.

The door opens, and I pause mid-stride as Joseph walks into the room. My lips part, and my breath halts.

My heart skips a beat at the sight of him. Dressed in dark slacks, a crisp, black dress shirt and coat, he looks pale and a little rough around the edges with a day's worth of coarse stubble around his jawline, but he's never looked so damn good to me. I'm so relieved to see him after being secluded in this room for hours.

"What's going on?" I ask him, immediately going to him.

He looks at me, holding me as I put my hands on his chest. But he doesn't answer me. My skin pricks with a chill. I know he's hiding a gunshot wound under his shirt. He has to be in pain. But I want to beat the shit out of him. Tell me what's going on!

I cross my arms over my chest, moving away from him and shoving the emotions down.

"You don't need to worry about it," he says finally, walking over to stand in front of Madam Lynn's desk. There's exhaustion in his voice, but he's doing his best to hide it. My eyes feel heavy and raw. I swallow thickly, not knowing what to do or say.

"You owe me more than that," I say warily. "You almost died. I –" I swallow thickly.

And now I'll never be the same. The room is filled with

nothing but the sound of my beating heart as he stares back at me, saying nothing. Offering me nothing.

I gesture sharply at him, pointing my finger at my chest. "I deserve to know."

Joseph shakes his head. "You don't need to know anything." His words are hard, but his eyes are soft. "I'm trying to keep you safe."

"Keeping me in the dark is not keeping me safe," I say with every ounce of sincerity I have.

When that doesn't get through to him, I add, "And I absolutely hate it here." I sound like a petulant child, and I hate it. But I really can't stand it here. I'd almost rather be in my fucking cage. And that's saying something.

His eyes study my face for a moment, and a twinge of hope goes through me. Maybe he'll change his mind. But when he speaks, his voice is firm. "It's the best place for you right now."

I start to argue with him when the door swings open, and in walks a man I met when Joseph brought me in here. Zander.

I turn in his direction, taking in his appearance. With chiseled features and dark blond hair, he's a handsome man, dressed in a black suit with a white dress shirt. Tall and noble-looking, but with eyes like his, he looks like he holds just as many secrets as Joseph does. It makes me wonder if this club is filled with men like them.

I guess it would make sense. Men like these don't become rich and powerful without accumulating secrets.

Joseph turns away from me to meet Zander's gaze. "What did you find out?" he asks him.

Zander glances at me for a moment, as if debating if he should talk in front of me. But Joseph gives him a slight nod to go ahead. The pain in my chest eases slightly at his gesture. At least he trusts me with some things.

WILLOW WINTERS & LAUREN LANDISH

"I know for a fact it was your brother," Zander says. Like Joseph, his voice is deep and rich, and it has a kind of calming quality to it. He stares at Joseph as if waiting for a violent reaction. "He set you up."

Joseph's quiet for a moment, and I can only wonder what he's feeling right now. His own brother tried to have him killed? It's not hard for me to comprehend after reading his journal. I know it still hurts him though. It makes my heart ache for him. I couldn't begin to comprehend being in such a position.

There's a coldness in Joseph's eyes that scares me when he answers, "I already know that." It reminds me of death.

"Good, then you'll be taking care of that matter soon?" Zander asks, taking a seat in the corner of the room as if they're talking about a sale on dry cleaning.

My heart skips a beat as I realize what this is about.

I don't even have to hear him say it. I know he's going to kill his own brother. His own flesh and blood. Joseph's answer is short, "Yes."

"When you go," Zander says, crossing his left ankle over his right knee, "check your father's closet." Zander's words are firm as he stares at Joseph with a hard look.

I stand there numb, not believing the casual tone of this conversation.

God, I feel sick. I walk slowly behind Joseph to the far end of the room, wishing I could disappear.

"I will," Joseph replies firmly.

Both men stare at each other for a moment, and then Zander gives Joseph a slight nod before leaving without another word.

As soon as the door clicks shut, I feel Joseph's eyes on me, waiting for my reaction.

"Please don't go," I plead, my voice nearly a croak, "you don't have to do this." My eyes are wide and begging for him to have mercy on me. I can't let him go. I don't know if he'll come back.

Joseph takes me in his arms, but he doesn't answer me. He holds onto me as I feel every last bit of hope slipping away. My nails dig into his shirt. "Please," I whisper. But there is no softening in his position. He's going whether I like it or not.

"I'll have tracking on my phone so you'll be able to see where I am," Joseph says, his voice soft, nearly sympathetic.

"I don't want to have to track you," I cry beneath my breath. "Just don't go! Please. Think about what you're about to do."

Joseph's voice remains firm. "I have. And that's why I have to do this." *Kill them.* The words seem to leap into my mind.

I sag against his firm body, tears burning my eyes. I don't want him to leave. I saw him shot, wounded and about to die. Now he's stepping in the line of danger again.

And it scares me like fuck that he might not come back. I cling onto him harder, feeling desperate and vulnerable and foolish, but I want him to stay. I want him to live. I can't save him if he leaves me.

"Please," I whisper against his hard chest as he tries hopelessly to soothe me. "I'm begging you."

Joseph's silent as he holds me.

"I have to go," Joseph tells me after a while, pulling back from me. Oh my God. It hurts like hell.

I try to cling to him, but he pries my fingers away from him, pushing me back against Madam Lynn's desk. I instantly feel cold. Abandoned.

"Let me go, Lilly," he says, his voice cold. God, he's breaking my heart. He's ripping it apart.

I shake my head, my throat throbbing from the aching pain. "No, you don't have to go."

"I'm leaving." His words are so cold now that I'm sure this

time he means it. I take a step back, wrapping my arms around myself and trying to hold myself together.

He gives me a kiss on the cheek that makes me close my eyes, the hot tears rolling down my cheeks. "I gave myself to you," I speak just above a murmur. He pauses at the door, his hand on the doorknob, and turns to look at me. My skin pricks under his gaze as the tears roll down my face.

I try to say more. I try to explain what I'm feeling. But all I can think about is the first night he took me. I brush away the bastard tears.

Through my hazy vision, I see Joseph staring back at me. He looks like he wants to tell me something. For the first time since he's walked in the room, I see something in his eyes. That same look I saw when he comforted me over Zach's death.

Tell me, I urge him silently. *Tell me that you love me.*

I want him to say it. Because I know I love him.

Say it! my mind screams.

And it looks like he's about to do it.

I part my lips expectantly, ready to say it back.

But then he turns away and walks out, not saying a word as he shuts the door behind him.

It's not till he's gone that I realize I never told him either. I whisper in the empty room. "I love you, Joseph. You better come back to me."

CHAPTER 28

Joseph

I STALK through the dark hallways of the home I grew up in. If one could call it a home. The memories that haunt my dreams flash before my eyes as my quiet footsteps cause the hardwood floors to creak beneath my boots.

I expected to be nervous. I anticipated my heart beating turbulently with a cold sweat swarming over my body. Instead there's nothing. I hold the handgun in my gloved hand, the silencer pointing down to the floor. As I step closer and closer to the room my brother stays in, I feel resolute.

The Levi household is practically a mansion. A lonely one, full of empty rooms. The screams when I grew up used to fill the halls, I'll never forget that. I know every inch of this place

I also know the escape route and where it leads. I learned it when I was young, it was something that we all needed to know. My father taught me the layout for my own safety. It's probably the one good thing he ever did for me. And now I'm using it against him.

I used the escape route to come into the kitchen, completely undetected. There are no alarms from there up to here, there's nothing standing in my way of creeping into their bedrooms and killing them in their sleep.

A small part of me wishes I would only kill my brother. My father never came after me. It's all my brother.

At the thought of leaving my father alive, my heart finally races and adrenaline courses through my blood. That's not something I can do. He will come for me. He may not know it was me, but he would come for me anyway. He would come to force me to take over the business. He's getting old, and there needs to be a Levi to carry on the name. But when the night is through, there will be none left.

I'll make sure of that.

I adjust my grip as I approach my brother's door, my heart pounding in my ears. All I need to do is shoot him in his sleep. He's an easy target, a simple kill. He deserves a much worse death. I'd like to wake him; I'd like to beat him into a bloody pulp with my bare hands.

Killing him this way isn't justice, but I can't afford risks.

Not when I have Lilly waiting for me.

I imagined his door will be locked, and testing the doorknob proves that much true. It doesn't take me long to pick it though. He was in the habit of locking his door when we grew up. He was also in the habit of stealing from me and of hurting women in the middle of the night. The memories flash before my eyes as the lock clicks, and the doorknob turns.

The memories make me sick. Not just because of what I've witnessed, but because of what I allowed to happen. I didn't have to; I could have fought. I would have lost, but I could have at least tried.

I open the door so slowly that it barely makes a sound. But every tiny noise forces my heart to jump in my chest. I know for a fact he'll have a gun near him. We all did growing up. That was the only way to ensure our safety. I can't afford to wake him.

I can barely breathe as I stalk into his room, placing each step as silently as possible. My eyes had already adjusted to the darkness in the hallway, and the faint light from his windows only adds to my ease of seeing in the dark.

The covers are loose around his hips. His body is visible, an easy target. I get closer than I need to, just to get a better look at him as I steal the life from him.

There's no bang to my gun. No sound other than the harsh breeze of the bullet whipping through the air. His body jolts once as the first bullet enters his head, and then another. And then another. I waste three bullets on him, staring at his dead body without feeling as though it's not real. The last two were unnecessary, only a result of my anger. Each time I pulled the trigger, I thought of the look on her face as she stared down at the man who tried to kill her. The man she killed. I put the gun to his head and pull the trigger again.

Looking down at my brother, even dead he looks cruel. There was never any hope for him, no saving him.

My father's next. It's the only thought in my mind, and the only thing that keeps me from putting a fifth bullet into Ricky's skull as I leave my brother's room. My father's suite is at the other end of the hallway. I don't hesitate to go to him next. My brother's death doesn't faze me in the least. If anything, it gives me more strength to put my father into the ground next to him. That's where they belong.

My heart stops when I walk into the room. Not needing to pick the lock, it opened easily. My feet halt when the floor creaks beneath my weight. I'm unsteady as I count two bodies in the bed. One is my father, and the closest to me.

His breathing is coming in heavy as he faintly snores in his sleep.

The other body is much smaller. A woman. And as the sound of my weight on the floorboards creaks through the night, she turns in her sleep. My heart beats erratically, my body heating and every tiny hair standing upright. I only planned on two deaths tonight. I don't want an innocent life caught in the crossfire. There's no way I can leave without seeing this through though. And I can't leave any witnesses.

I take one more step, pointing my gun at my father. I'm a few feet away, but all I need to do is put a bullet in his skull and I can leave, leaving the woman unharmed. *She doesn't have to die.*

My heart refuses to beat as the one last step I take is enough to wake the woman. She groans, stretching her arms and sitting up in the bed with a sleepy yawn, her eyes closed tight. Fuck! She rubs the sleep from her eyes as I take two steps forward.

The sound of my jeans scraping against one another fills the room and wakes her further. The silencer points directly at my father's head; I get one bullet off before the woman screams. It's all I need though. My father's head jolts as the bullet leaves a neat hole just to the right of the center of his forehead.

I can't think; I can't breathe. My body feels like it's heating to an unbearable degree. I don't know how I can save her. As I try to think, she does something she should know not to do. She turns her back to me, grabbing the gun off the nightstand. She grips it with both hands, turning toward me, ready to shoot me.

And for a split second I consider letting her.

What good have I done the world? Killing my father and brother were the last good things I could ever do. The best things I've done with my life. I've lived with no purpose for years.

The sound of her pulling the hammer back, the cold steel shaking in her trembling hands, loading the barrel of the gun with the bullet she intends to kill me with, triggers the memory of her, Lilly. Of my flower.

I need to live for her.

Without another thought, I pull the trigger. The bullet whizzes through the air, hitting her in her throat. She falls off the bed, the gun leaving her hand and falling with a thump onto the padded carpet.

I'm quick to go to her side, now that she's unarmed. I kick the gun to the side as both of her hands press against her throat, trying to stop the blood. My initial reaction is to save her. I kneel on the ground; she looks at me with wide eyes filled with fear. I press my palm to the wound in her neck even as she tries to helplessly push me away. The woman has fight, but there's too much blood. It pains my heart. I didn't want this.

"I'm sorry," I barely get the words out as her hot blood covers both of my gloved hands and soaks into the cream carpet.

I stare down at the dying woman. Her innocent blood is on my hands as I try to stop the wound from gushing blood. The pumps of hot liquid become weaker and weaker as her heart slows, and the life falls from her eyes. One deep breath leaves her, and she's gone. Another victim. I don't know who she is, but her death is on my hands.

The sick fuck that my father is, he had to tie me to a chair before he did it. I struggle against the binds at my wrists, but it's useless. My ankles are bound, and my thighs are strapped to the chair beneath me. So is my chest. I scream until my throat is raw and hoarse. For the first time in my life, my cheeks are wet with tears.

He's punishing me for not doing his will. For disobeying an order. I was trying to do what was right. I was trying to save the woman he wanted me to torture. And now I have no choice but to watch as he beats my mother in front of me. I look up at my brother, pleading with him to help.

"He's killing her!" I scream at him. Mother isn't even crying anymore. At first, she tried not to scream. She didn't want to see me upset. She told me it was okay. She told me she loved me. Even as my father slapped her across the face with the butt of the gun. But as he continued, his brutal hits coming with more force, she couldn't hold it back any longer. She begged him, just as I am now.

My brother looks back at me with the same look that my father's always had. Eyes filled with malice. The breath leaves my lungs, and my voice is lost as a shrill bang echoes in the small room. I hang my head low.

I was only twelve, and that was the last time anyone called me little sparrow. And the last time anyone told me they loved me.

I look down at the woman one last time, wiping her blood on the sheets as I stand, towering over her and glancing back at my father. Her eyes are closed, and she's covered in blood. My father's eyes are open and cold and that's how they always were, staring at nothing. Beneath him blood pools into the mattress. The sheet soaks up the dark red liquid.

She may have died because I came tonight. To finish this.

I almost leave without heeding Zander's words, that I need to check the closet. My eyes dart to the double doors, and I take cautious steps to see what lies behind them. My body heats, knowing I'm trusting him. A man I don't know.

The door squeaks open slowly, the only sound in the room other than my own shallow breathing. The blood rushes in my ears, drowning out all other sounds as I stare at the monitors and video recordings of every inch of this house. Some areas I don't recognize. The screens flicker and move to rooms I've never seen before. It's surveillance, of this house and of somewhere else.

I watch them for a moment, each second passing, my body chills and my heart pounds. I remove the tapes, one by one. There are eight of them, and I stop the recordings before leaving. Had Zander not told me, there's no doubt in my mind I would've gone away for murder this time. The hard evidence is undeniable.

I walk to the door, stepping over the poor woman's dead body and turning my back to my father.

It's over now.

And not another body will be put in the ground because of that man. I close the door behind me and leave the way I came.

CHAPTER 29

Lilly

I'VE BEEN TOSSING and turning all night. The back of my eyes is throbbing from a terrible headache, brought on by a lack of sleep. I think I've been up for over twenty-four hours, running on fumes.

I'm in a private room at Club X. The bed I'm lying on, a king-size plush pillow top mattress, is soft and comfortable. It practically begs me to go to sleep. But I can't. It's nice and all, but I prefer my room back at Joseph's house. Or his room, as long as he's next to me.

I can't stop thinking about him. I don't know if he's okay, or if he's even alive.

I swallow thickly as I see the dim light of morning peeking around the luxury curtains and then glance at the phone he left me.

The little dot that tracks his location is in the same spot. It makes me feel sick, like something's terribly wrong. The fucking dot won't move. I wish I could talk to someone-- Joseph, or one of his associates, and be assured that he's okay. Anyone!

I called his phone at least a dozen times, but he hasn't answered. I knew he wouldn't in the beginning, but by now he should've.

My throat constricts and I roll over in bed, hating to think about it. Hating time for going so slowly.

Just come back to me.

A knock on the door brings me to my feet faster than I would have thought possible, my heart pounding in my chest.

I'm just at the door when Madam Lynn walks in.

She looks sharp as usual, dressed in a black dress that has ruffles at the bottom and black glossy heels, her hair pulled up into an elegant bun while wispy bangs frame her face. She looks perfectly fine. As though her friend isn't out killing his father and brother this very second.

Her face is solemn as she steps into the room and stops a few feet away from me.

"I'm here to tell you that you can go home now," Madam Lynn says softly. "Isaac set up a security system around your townhouse. You don't need it," she shakes her head gently, her eyes rolling as she adds, "He's peculiar about safety."

I part my lips to ask her about Joseph when there's a knock at the door.

Isaac sticks his head through the doorway, glances between the both of us, and then steps inside the room. Though I'm filled with anxiety, I can't help but notice the authority Isaac radiates. It reminds me of Joseph. Those chis-eled features, the power and ruthlessness behind his eyes are familiar to me.

"It's done," Isaac tells Madam Lynn. "I've made sure that no one will gain access."

The look that passes across Madam Lynn's face as she glances at Isaac is one of extreme gratitude.

"But what about Joseph?" I ask. The hell with my safety, I want to know what's going on.

Madam Lynn exchanges a glance with Isaac and something seems to silently pass between them. My heart pounds harder in my chest.

I look back and forth between the both of them. "Where is he?" My body trembles with anxiety. Someone tell me something!

Madam Lynn is silent, and the look of sadness she throws my way makes my stomach churn.

"Please tell me what's going on!" I cry.

"You're better off without him," Isaac says finally, firmly. At the frown that crumples my face, he adds, "I'm sorry if it's not what you want to hear, but he's no good for you, Lilly."

"Isaac!" Madam Lynn snaps, and she looks pissed. And Isaac's shocked.

"If he really wanted you, he'd be here. Not leaving you to wonder where he's at," Isaac says.

"That's not true. You don't know him!" I cry out.

"Get out, Isaac," Madam Lynn says in a low voice. "I told you, you don't know him." Her voice is full of hurt. And from the look that flashes in his eyes, he seems genuinely sorry.

"Out," Madam Lynn says in a bit of a brighter tone, shooing him away.

Isaac stands there for a moment waiting for her to look at him again, but she doesn't. He looks like he wants to tell me something. But again... nothing.

He presses his lips into a straight line and nods before leaving the room. At the door, he stops to tell me, "My team and I will be waiting to escort you home, Ms. Wade. Just come to us when you're ready."

I don't answer him. Fuck him for saying that. It hurts. I'm

already hurting, and what he said was only salt in the wound. The only words I can get out are, "You don't know him."

The second the door closes, Madam Lynn says, "I was really pissed at Joseph." She clears her throat, taking the seat in the far corner of the room. The chair is a pale pink, and studded nails line the smooth leather. She runs her hands down the edge and it suits her. She looks like she belongs there.

"He's okay," she says and I stare at her with wide eyes. "Joseph is." My body sags with relief. "He called a few hours ago. It's over with."

A few hours ago? Her words hit me like a knife to my back.

"I'm sorry about Isaac. He doesn't know Joseph well." I can tell she's trying to change the subject, but I don't let her.

"Hours?" I ask her. Her expression tells me that she knows how I feel.

"He's safe. And he knows you're safe." I'm quiet as I sit on the edge of the bed, overwhelmed by so many emotions.

"He'll come for you. I'm sure he will." Her eyes are so full of sincerity, that I believe her. I believe that she truly thinks he will.

But her words don't give me the confidence I need. I want him here now. I want to watch that stupid dot on the phone coming closer and closer to me. Bringing him back to me.

But then I think back to the last look he gave me, and my doubts fall away.

I know what I saw in his eyes. And that wasn't a lie.

He loves me. And he's going to come for me.

And if he doesn't, then I'll go to him.

CHAPTER 30

Joseph

THE TRUNK CLOSES at the foot of my bed with a loud clack. All the memories of my past have been placed inside, including my journal. I have no need for it anymore, no desire to write another word.

It's over.

There's not a single target on my back with both my father and my brother gone. Zander's assured me he'll keep his ear low to the ground. His finger's on the pulse of what's going on behind closed doors. I'm not sure what he wants from me, he's yet to ask. I don't like owing a debt to anyone if I can help it, but still I'm grateful.

Because of Lilly.

I want her back. I want her here, in my house and in my bed, just like I did that first night I saw her. She belongs to me now. So any protection I can take, I will. Even if that means making a deal with Zander.

As I grab my keys, they clink off the foyer table. The sound echoes with me as I realized the only reason I'll be coming home without her is if she doesn't want me. My hand hesitates on the doorknob, my mind replaying all the moments we've had in the past month.

We've grown together. I've been there for her, and she's been there for me. At least in my mind, that's what happened. I know these past two weeks she's been a prisoner, unable to go as she pleases. It was for her own safety, her own good. As I close the front door behind me, my body heats as I remember her in the cage staring at me with daggers in her eyes.

She could leave me now. She could walk away from me forever, and there's nothing I can do. I never locked the cage, and I never will.

The thought chills me along with the bitter cold February air. I forgot my coat. I don't give a fuck; I'm not going back. Not until I have her in my arms.

My strides quicken, and I hit the clicker to unlock my car. The faint *beep beep* rings out in the cold.

I'll be coming back with my flower. I know I will.

Just as I open my driver door, I see a car coming up the long winding drive. There's a dusting of snow over the clearing, and as the old red Honda takes the bend, the car drifts slightly.

My heart races in my chest, and I drop the keys onto the ground.

Lilly.

She regains control and takes it slower up the drive. I swear to God if she kills herself finding her way back to me, I'll never forgive her.

I leave the keys where they are as small specks of snow float down from the sky and Lilly parks her car in the driveway. She looks up through the windshield, hesitation clear on her face, that gorgeous vulnerability shining in her doe eyes.

My flower.

I try not to assume that she's come for me. That once again we desire the same thing. A harsh lump forms in my throat, the spikes threatening to suffocate me. My hands clench and unclench as the chill of the air starts to affect me.

I ignore all of it, walking to her driver door and opening it. She looks up at me warily as I offer her my hand. *Please don't deny me, my flower.* Be here for me. Please.

Her hand feels so small, so warm in mine. I've always known we were different, but I've grown to love how she complements me. She brings out a side to me that I don't want to lose.

We share a look, I'm not sure what mine reflects to her, but hers undeniably sends a chill through my body. She's looking at me as though she doesn't know what I'm thinking. I've seen it on her face a dozen times or more.

She should know what she means to me. And the fact that she doesn't makes me nervous. I'm not a man who likes to be nervous. It's not a comfortable feeling.

My hand splays on the small of her back, but I'm quick to pull her in close, wrapping my arm around her waist and holding her small body into mine as I lead her inside.

When I peek down at her, lowering myself to the ground to pick up my keys that are now freezing and coated with a thin layer of snow, I see a small smile on her lips. Nothing in my life has made me feel better. She makes me feel secure and wanted. I'll never let her go. Never. When you find someone who makes you feel like this, there's no reason to ever give her a reason to walk away.

She shivers in the doorway as I unlock the door, opening it and allowing the warmth of my home to spread through us both. Her heels click in the foyer as she continues walking without me. I close the door with my back to her, taking a deep breath. She came back to me. I can't let her leave. I close my eyes at that thought, realizing that's not what she needs. I need to give her a reason to stay of her own free will. I can't keep her here, but knowing that she's come here has to mean something.

I turn slowly to face her, her ankles cross slightly and she sways, standing there in the middle of the open doorway, her hands clasped and her coat hanging in the crook of her arm. She looks just as nervous as I feel. The sight of her reminds me of the first day I had her here. The same uncertainty, and just like before I know I'll soothe her worries. If only she lets me.

"I want you to stay for another month," I offer her, my voice echoes off the empty walls, walking to her and standing just inches in front of her. Technically our contract isn't over yet; Valentine's Day is tomorrow. But I want to bind her with the contract if I can. I don't want the days to pass and have no claim to her.

"Just a month?" she asks, a look flashing in her eyes. I like hearing the words "Yes, Sir" from her lips. But this may be even better.

"You want more, my flower?" I hope she says yes. Whatever she tells me she wants, I'll give her. I just need her to tell me.

I finally feel like I have a reason to live. And a future to look forward to with Lilly. I can give her whatever she needs. Whatever she asks for, I would happily provide her with. I'm sure she's realized that by now. Without her with me, I was clinging to the past just to feel. I don't want that anymore. I want her; all of her.

"I care for you Lilly," I stare into her eyes as I tell her, for the first time I think in my entire life making my feelings known for someone else. I feel vulnerable in this moment, and she looks back at me, not answering. She could reject me. It would crush me if she did.

My thumb rubs along her cheek as I cup her chin in my hand. Her hands gently wrap around my wrists as she leans into my touch. Her eyes close, and a look of pure happiness is on her face. It soothes the worry in me, but still I need her to tell me that she feels the same. I know the way we started wasn't what she wanted. It was a game of fools thinking we each knew what we wanted, when we knew nothing. But now I know. And I'm ready to fight for her.

"You can say you love me. I know you do," Lilly says teasingly.

Finally opening her pale blue eyes, it's as though she's looking straight into my soul. The look in her eyes doesn't match the tone of her voice. She needs me to tell her. I'm not sure if I'd recognize the emotion love. It's not something I grew up with, nothing I've ever felt before. But there's something different between the two of us. Something that drew me to her that first day. And something that fuels me to move mountains to be with her. To never let her go.

"I love you, Lilly." My lips brush against hers as I whisper the words. It must be love. "I love you."

"I love you, Sir."

HER WRISTS ARE BOUND by the thin rope, the end looped over the cast-iron loop above the headboard. She's bound to my bed where she belongs. Her movements are easy. The only reason the ropes are even there is to prevent her from spearing her fingers in my hair as I continue to lick between her legs. Her arousal is so sweet, so delicious. And all mine.

I crawl up her body, kissing my way as I go. Her thighs wrap around my shoulders and then down my sides to my waist. I've given her as much control as she can manage for this session. No holding still. No asking permission. All she has to do is feel and react. Although I did bind her wrists... she's greedy.

My fingers are wrapped around her throat as I settle my hips between her thighs, spreading her even more. My hard dick nestles between her sweet pussy. I kiss her lips with the intense passion I feel. I'm grateful for every moment with her. I'll never let her go. I need her too much.

"Who do you belong to?" I ask her.

"You, Sir, only you." I love how lust coats her voice.

"Only me for always," I tell her before slamming into her, all the way to the hilt, capturing her cries of pleasure with my lips. The headboard knocks against the wall with each hard thrust. It only fuels me to take her harder.

She is my one and only. And I'm hers.

EPILOGUE

Lilly

"NOT THIS BULLSHIT AGAIN!" I slam the book that I'm reading, *Don't Stop,* shut with a frustrated growl. How in the hell did I manage to find another book that pisses me off so much that I want to throw it across the room? And after I took every precaution to make sure I didn't?

This one was even worse than the last. The hero and heroine, Randy and Ada, made it through so many trials and tribulations that I was rooting for them like crazy toward the end.

I got really excited, turning the pages with bated breath. And it looked like their path was on its way to glory, only to find out that Ada was hiding a secret baby from Randy. A baby that was sure to cause major scandal between their families. The book cut off right there.

Ugh. It makes me so mad!

Like, who the fuck does that?

I can't say it enough.

I. Detest. Cliffhangers.

But even after all that, I'm dying to know what happened.

A thousand poxes on the author for doing this to me and making me wait! ...I know I'll end up buying the next one though. I blow a strand of hair out of my face as I toss the book onto the ottoman. I guess I'm a glutton for punishment.

I stretch out before grabbing my laptop and opening up my manuscript.

Last night I rewarded myself with writing a chapter of my new novel when I was finally finished my grueling lesson plans.

I'm excited about *both* the classes and my book.

The words for the novel are flowing easily. And I know with all the inspiration that I have, and the support of my awesome beta reader Jenna, I'll be able to do the book justice.

But it's my hobby. Not my job. I chew my bottom lip, holding back my smile. I got my old job back before the semester even started. Some anonymous donor came through and funded the *Children in Need Foundation*.

Anonymous. Joseph actually started to tell me it wasn't him when I pried. He didn't want me to feel like I owed him. He has no idea how much I owe him. But not in the way he thinks.

I can't believe how much he's helped me in the short time we've been together. How much we've helped each other. And lately, I've been able to have both sides to him, the Master and the gentleman.

A soft sigh escapes my lips at the thought.

Just thinking about it, I can't imagine my life getting any better.

The sound of heavy footsteps in the doorway causes me to look up, and my heart skips a beat at the dangerously sexy man who's standing there.

"Reading something?" his deep masculine voice asks.

Wearing dark grey dress pants and a white Henley open at the chest, his hair slicked to the side, Joseph looks like an absolute vision as he leans against the doorway with a grin on his face.

"Sir," I practically purr as he pulls away from the door and walks into the room.

I slip out of my chair and onto my knees, getting down on all floors and crawling forward like a vixen.

Joseph chuckles playfully at the sight. He's told me to do this when I want to play with him, and I take full advantage.

"Up," he orders me.

I rise to my feet and look him in the eye. Up close, I'm enveloped by that masculine scent that I love so much, and I inhale deeply, sucking in as much of him as I can.

Grinning, he wraps my arms around his waist and pulls me in close, delivering a soft kiss to my lips.

"I was," I reply to his earlier question when he pulls back, leaving me breathless.

He chuckles again. "I know. I could hear you yelling from across the house."

My cheeks turn red with embarrassment. I hadn't realized I'd been yelling like a maniac. But I guess that's what happens when you get smacked in the face with a cliffhanger.

"Sorry," I mutter.

Joseph quirks an amused eyebrow. "What happened in it that got you so worked up?"

"You don't want to know," I growl.

Joseph pouts. "That's not fair."

Neither was that ending. I still want to beat that author's ass like they're a Submissive from Club X. I don't bother saying it though.

"Life isn't fair," I say, giving him another kiss on the lips.

Joseph grins at me.

We stare at each other for a moment, and my heart feels full. I can't believe how lucky that I am to have this man.

"What?" I ask, breaking out of my thoughts to see Joseph gazing at me with a mischievous smile.

"I've got something for you."

My heart stalling in my chest, I watch as he produces a large, black velvet box. For a moment, I think it might be an engagement ring, but the box is far too big.

A faint smile spreads across my face and I shake my head at my eagerness. It's too soon to be expecting something like that. But I do want it. I want everyone to know that he's mine, and I'm his.

It will happen, I tell myself. *Eventually.*

I clear my throat, reaching out for it, and our fingers brush against one another and I feel that same spark I felt so long ago. Maybe not that long ago, but it feels like it with everything we've been through.

"Open it," he prods softly, pushing the box into my hands.

I keep the smile on my face although my throat closes, and I do as he says. My heart jumps when I see what's inside, my knees going weak.

"Joseph," I gasp, my eyes filling with tears, the air being pulled from my lungs. *Oh my God, oh my God,* I repeat in my mind over and over.

It's a collar, a beautiful one, black and silver, encrusted with sparkling diamonds. But it isn't the first thing that caught my eye.

There's a ring in there, too. I choke on my words for a moment, in shock but mostly just overwhelmed with so much happiness.

"What's this?" I somehow manage, my voice a breathless whisper, though I know exactly what it is. Staring at the ring, a platinum band with a large, sparkling diamond atop of it, it's suddenly very hard to breathe.

I imagined it moments before, but this doesn't seem real.

Joseph sinks to his knee in front of me, his heart in his eyes. My heart skips a beat and my skin pricks as reality sets in. The room spins around me as I stare down at him, and I feel like passing out.

"Lilly Marie Wade, my flower," he says, his voice aching with emotion, "Will you marry me?"

I stare at him in disbelief, my throat so tight with emotion I'm barely able to fill my lungs. I can't find the words to answer. I'm stunned.

The silence stretches on for several long moments as I try to get over my shock. My chest heaves as I struggle to draw in breaths, my legs feeling like jello. Through it all, Joseph waits patiently, staying on one knee.

Say yes, you idiot!

"Yes!" I'm finally able to croak when I find my voice, leaning down to wrap my arms around his neck and bury his face with tearful kisses, my heart pounding like a battering ram. "Yes, yes, yes! I'll marry you, Joseph!"

"Good." Joseph pulls me down into his arms, delivering a deep solid kiss to my lips. "Because I love you, Lilly. And I'm never letting you go."

I smile up at him through my tears, my heart aching from the unbelievable joy that fills my body and the happiness I see reflected in his eyes.

Delivering another kiss to his lips, I breathe out through aching lungs, "I love you too, Joseph."

Want more? Continue reading for a sneak peek of the fourth book, Given, Zander's story!

Join our mailing list to receive bonus deleted scenes! (If you're already on our lists, you'll get this automatically).

Ooh and I would love to show you a preview of Merciless! I'm currently obsessed with this world and I'd love for you to get a sneak peek! - Willow xx

Keep reading at the end, I've included a sneak peek into my novel, Dirty Talk. I think you'll love it! - Lauren xo

GIVEN: HIGHEST BIDDER
BOOK 4

PROLOGUE

ZANDER

Both of my hands tremble, and the adrenaline pumping in my blood makes my muscles coil, ready to fight. I grip the edge of the dresser to keep my body upright. I only need to breathe. A long and slow exhale leaves me, lowering my tense shoulders. I crack my neck before looking over my shoulder at her. *My sweetheart.*

I've never run from anything in my life. And I'm not about to start now.

But I should have run from *her*. I knew I should have walked away when I first laid eyes on her.

She's destroyed my control. Ruined my reputation. She'll be the end of me, I know it.

Her soft moans of pain from across the bedroom call to me. She's so beautifully broken. She *needs* me.

I took it too far, and I can't take it back.

They'll come for me. I'm certain the cops will be here soon. I'm guilty, and I have no one to blame. The evidence is all right here, and I can't deny a damn thing.

For the first time in my life, I don't see a way out.

There's no one I can turn to. No one who owes me who can make this right.

But I can't stop wanting her. She's gotten under my skin. And I won't stop fighting for her.

Never.

"Zander," she says, and her small voice is choked. Her brow is pinched as her head thrashes from side to side and the doctor works on the deep lashes on her back. Agony rises through my chest and stiffens my body. My eyes burn and my throat closes as I try to breathe.

She's stripped to the waist, lying face down on the bed, her bottom half barely covered by a thin white sheet to keep the doctor's prying eyes from seeing even more of her.

I know what he thinks. What they all think since I took her.

I don't give a fuck. I pay him well to turn a blind eye, and that's exactly what he'll do. It's what they all do. They only want the money, and they'll do anything for it.

But not her.

The plush rug softens my heavy footsteps as I cross the master bedroom and walk to her. She lifts her head as I come closer, but the moment she does, she winces and sucks in a reluctant breath through clenched teeth.

I'm quick to gentle my hand on her shoulder, keeping my contact confined to the small area of soft skin without any wounds. "Don't move," I say, and my voice is low, admonishing even. I hate myself. I'm so devoid of the ability to comfort that I can't even speak softly to her when she's . . . like this.

"I'm sorry," Arianna says quietly, her voice muffled from the mattress.

A chill runs over every inch of my skin. She has no reason to apologize to me. She never did anything wrong. Not since the first moment this started.

236

I swallow thickly, and the lump forming in my throat feels as though it scratches the tender skin on the way down. "It's all right." I try to soften my voice and put as much warmth into it as possible. I pet her hair with soothing strokes.

"I never should have left you," Arianna replies, her words coming out slow and full of genuine remorse.

She shouldn't have. This wouldn't have happened if she'd just listened. If she'd *trusted* me.

But it's my fault. Not hers.

"It's going to be all right," I say softly, crouching down so my eyes are level with hers. It's a lie. It's not going to be all right. I'm damn sure of that single truth. Everything is fucked.

But I'll tell her whatever she needs to hear.

I can't lose her.

I press my lips to hers, my hand cupping her jaw and my thumb rubbing comforting circles on her soft skin.

"Is it going to be okay?" she whispers against my lips. It's only when I open my eyes and see that hers are still closed with tears running freely down her reddened cheeks that my heart shatters.

I wish I could tell her I'll take care of everything.

But it's not okay. And I can't fix this.

I know I shouldn't, but lying comes so easily to me. "Everything's going to be fine," I tell her. Her long lashes flutter and her gorgeous green eyes open to look back at me. So much raw vulnerability and something else are clearly evident in her gaze. Something that should push me away.

I didn't even want to take her when she was first given to me. I should have refused.

Maybe even then, I recognized what she would do to me. How she would change who I am and destroy everything I've worked for. When they put me behind bars, they'll figure out everything. The corruption, the money, all the lies.

Even knowing that, I wouldn't hesitate to take her if I had the chance to do it all over again. My hand clenches into a fist, firming my resolve. Even if I couldn't change a damn thing, I'd still accept that sick fuck's offer.

She was given to me.

Now she's *mine*.

CLICK HERE TO KEEP READING GIVEN!

SNEAK PEEK AT MERCILESS

From *USA Today* bestselling author W Winters comes a heart-wrenching, edge-of-your-seat gripping, romantic suspense.

I should've known she would ruin me the moment I saw her.
　Women like her are made to destroy men like me.
　I couldn't resist her though.
　Given to me to start a war; I was too eager to accept.

But I didn't know what she'd do to me. That she would change everything.
　She sees through me in a way no one else ever has.
　Her innocence and vulnerability make me weak for her and I hate it.

I know better than to give in to temptation.

A ruthless man doesn't let a soul close to him.

A cold-hearted man doesn't risk anything for anyone.

A powerful man with a beautiful woman at his mercy …
he doesn't fall for her.

CHAPTER 1

CARTER

*W*ar is coming.

It's something I've known for over two years.

Tick. Tock. Tick. Tock.

My jaw ticks in time with the skin over my knuckles turning white as my fist clenches tighter. The tension in my stiff shoulders rises and I have to remind myself to breathe in deep and let the strain of it all go away.

Tick. Tock. It's the only sound echoing off the walls of my office and with each passing of the pendulum the anger grows.

It's always like this before I go to a meet. This one in particular sends a thrill through my blood, the adrenaline pumping harder with each passing minute.

My gaze moves from the grandfather clock in my office to the shelves next to it and then beneath them to the box made of mahogany and steel. It's only three feet deep and tall and six feet long. It blends into the right wall of my office, surrounded by polished bookshelves that carry an aroma of old books.

I paid more than I should have simply to put on display. All any of this is a façade. People's perceptions are their reality. And so I paint the picture they need to see so I can use them as I see fit. The expensive books and paintings, polished furniture made of rare wood... All of it is bullshit.

Except for the box. The story that came with it will stay with me forever. In all of the years, it's the one of the few memories that I can pin point as a defining moment. The box never leaves me.

The words from the man who gave it to me are still as clear as is the memory of his pale green eyes, glassed over as he told me his story.

About how it kept him safe when he was a child. He told me how his mother had shoved him in it to protect him.

I swallow thickly, feeling my throat tighten and the cord in my neck strain with the memory. He painted the picture so well.

He told me how he clung to his mother seeing how panicked she was. But he did as he was told, he stayed quiet in the safe box and could only listen while the men murdered his mother.

It was the story he gave me with the box he offered to barter for his life. And it reminded me of my own mother telling me goodbye before she passed.

Yes, his story was touching, but the defining moment is when I put the gun to his head and pulled the trigger regardless.

He tried to steal from me and then pay me with a box as if the money he laundered was a debt or a loan. William was good at stealing, at telling stories, but the fucker was a dumb prick.

I didn't get to where I am by playing nicely and being weak. That day I took the box that saved him as a reminder of who I was. Who I needed to be.

I made sure that box has been within my sight for every meeting I've had in this office. It's a reminder for me so I can stare at it in this god forsaken room as I make deal after deal with criminal after criminal and collect wealth and power like the dusty old books on these shelves.

It cost me a fortune to get this office exactly how I wanted. But if it were to burn down, I could buy it all over again.

Everything except for that box.

"You really think they're going through with it?" I hear Daniel, my brother, before I see him. The memories fade in an instant and my heart beat races faster than the tick tock of that fucking clock.

It takes a second for me to be conscious of my facial expression, to relax it and let go of the anger before I can raise my gaze to his.

"With the war and the deal? You think he'll go through with it?" he clarifies.

A small huff leaves me, accompanied by a smirk, "He wants this more than anything else," I answer him.

Daniel stalks into the room slowly, the heavy door to my office closing with a soft kick of his heel before he comes to stand across from me.

"And you're sure you want to be right in the middle of it?"

I lick my lower lip and stand from my desk, stretching as I do and turning my gaze to the window in my office. I can hear Daniel walking around the desk as I lean against it and cross my arms.

"We won't be in the middle of it. It'll be the two of them, our territory is close, but we can stay back."

"Bullshit. He wants you to fight with him and he's going to start this war tonight and you know it."

I nod slowly, the smell of Romano's cigars filling my lungs at the memory of him.

"There's still time to call it off," Daniel says and it makes my brow pinch and place a crease on my forehead. He can't be that naïve.

It's the first time I've really looked at him since he's been back. He spent years away. And every fucking day I fought for what we have. He's gone soft. Or maybe it's Addison that's turned him into the man standing in front of me.

"This war has to happen." My words are final and the tone is one not to be questioned. I may have grown this business on fear and anger. Each step forward followed by the hollow sound of a body dropping behind me, but that's not how it started. Y can't build an empire with blood stained hands and not expect death to follow you.

His dark eyes narrow as he pushes off the desk and moves closer to the window, his gaze flickering between me and the meticulously maintained garden stories below us.

"Are you sure you want to do this?" his voice is low and I barely hear it. He doesn't look back at me and a chill flows down my arms and the back of my neck as I take in his stern expression.

It takes me back years ago. Back to when we had a choice and chose wrong.

When whether or not we wanted to go through with it meant something.

"There are men to the left of us," I tell him as I step forward and close the distance between us. "There are men to the right. There is no possible outcome where we don't pick a side."

He nods once and slides his thumb across the stubble on his chin before looking back at me. "And the girl?" he asks me, his eyes piercing into mine and reminding me that both of us survived, both of us fought, and each of us has a tragic path that led us to where we are today.

"Aria?" I dare to speak her name and the sound of my

smooth voice seems to linger in the space between us. I don't wait for him to acknowledge me, or her rather.

"She has no choice." My voice tightens as I say the words.

Clearing my throat, I lean my palms against the window, feeling the frigid fall beneath my hands and leaning forward to see Addison beneath us, Daniel's Addison. "What do you think they would have done to Addison if they'd succeeded in taking her?"

His jaw hardens but he doesn't answer my question. Instead he replies, "We don't know who it was who tried to take her from me."

I shrug as if it's semantics and not at all relevant. "Still. Women aren't meant to be touched, but they went for Addison first."

"That doesn't make it right," Daniel says with indignation in his tone.

"Isn't it better she come to us?" My head tilts as I question him and this time he takes a moment to respond.

"She's not one of us. Not like Addison and you know what Romano expects you to do with her."

"Yes, the daughter of the enemy…" My heart beats hard in my chest, and the steady rhythm reminds me of the ticking of the clock. "I know exactly what he wants me to do with her."

Click here to keep reading Merciless!

SNEAK PEEK AT DIRTY TALK

He makes dirty sound so good. So right.

The moment I heard his velvety voice growl that I'm his 'Kitty Kat', I knew I was in trouble.

Derrick 'The Love Whisperer' King gives out relationship and sex advice on the radio to everyone, but he's giving me something a bit more personal. Nobody's ever talked to me the way he does. Daring, Demanding, Sexy... and oh, so **Dirty**.

Maybe we started this whole thing a little backward, sex first and getting to know each other after. But I'm starting to let my guard down, my untrusting heart beginning to think that maybe fairy tales do come true. Even for me.

I feel beautiful and hopeful when he worships my body. I feel dirty and naughty when he whispers filthy things in my ear.

But is it real? Can something so naughty **really** be good for me?

And more importantly, against all odds, can it last… **forever**?

Dirty Talk is a full-length Romance with a happy ever after, no cheating, and no cliffhanger!

EXCERPT

KATRINA

"*C*heckmate, bitch," I exclaim as I do a victory dance that's comprised of fist pumps and ass wiggles in my chair while my best friend Elise laughs at me. I turn in my seat and start doing a little half-stepping Rockettes dance. "Can-can, I just kicked some can-can, I so am the wo-man, and I rule this place!"

Elise does a little finger dance herself, cheering along with me. "You go, girl. Winner, winner, chicken dinner. Now let's eat!"

I laugh with her, joyful in celebrating my new promotion at work, regardless of the dirty looks the snooty ladies at the next table are shooting our way. I get their looks. I mean, we are in the best restaurant in the city. While East Robinsville isn't New York or Miami, we're more of a Northeastern suburb of . . . well, everything in between. This just isn't the sort of restaurant where five-foot-two-inch women in work clothes go shaking their ass while chanting something akin to a high school cheer.

But right now, I give exactly zero fucks. "Damn right, we can eat! I'm the youngest person in the company to ever be promoted to Senior Developer and the first woman at that level. Glass ceiling? Boom, busting through! Boys' club? Infiltrated." I mime like I'm sneaking in, shoulders hunched and hands pressed tightly in front of me before splaying my arms wide with a huge grin. "Before they know it, I'm gonna have that boys' club watching chick flicks and the whole damn office is going to be painted pink!"

Elise snorts, shaking her head again. "I still don't have a fucking clue what you actually do, but even I understand the words *promotion* and *raise*. So huge congrats, honey."

She's right, no one really understands when I talk about my job. My brain has a tendency to talk in streams of binary zeroes and ones that make perfect sense to me, but not so much to the average person. When I was in high school, I even dreamed in Java.

And even I don't really understand what my promotion means. Senior Developer? Other than the fact that I get updated business cards with my fancy new title next week, I'm not sure what's changed. I'm still doing my own coding and my own work, just with a slightly higher pay grade. And when I say slightly, I mean barely a bump after taxes. Just enough for a bonus cocktail at a swanky club on Friday maybe. *Maybe* more at year end, they'd said. Ah, well, I'm excited anyway. It's a first step and an acknowledgement of my work.

The part people do get is when my company turns my strings of code into apps that go viral. After my last app went number one, they were forced to give me a promotion or risk losing my skills to another development company. They might not understand the zeroes and ones, but everyone can grasp dollars and cents, and that's what my apps bring in.

I might be young at only twenty-six, and female, as evidenced by my long honey-blonde hair and curvy figure, but as much as I don't fit the stereotypical profile of a computer nerd, they had to respect that my brain creates things that no one else does. I think it's my female point of view that really helps. While a chunk of the other people in the programming field fit the stereotype of being slightly repressed geeks who are more comfortable watching animated 'girlfriends' than talking to an actual woman, I'm different. I understand that merely slapping a pink font on things or adding sparkly shit and giving more pre-loaded shopping options doesn't make technology more 'female-friendly.'

It's insulting, honestly. But it gives me an edge in that I know how to actually create apps that women like and want to use. Not just women, either, based on sales. I'm getting a lot of men downloading my apps too, especially men who aren't into tech-geeking out every damn thing they own.

And so I celebrate with Elise, holding up our glasses of wine and clinking them together in a toast. Elise sips her wine and nods in appreciation, making me glad we went with the waiter's recommendation. "So you're killing it on the job front. What else is going on? How are things with you and Kevin?"

Elise has been my best friend since we met at a college recruiting event. She's all knockout looks and sass, and I'm short, nervous, and shy in professional situations, but we clicked. She knows I've been through the wringer with some previous boyfriends, and even though Kevin is fine—well-mannered, ambitious, and treats me right—she just doesn't care for him for some reason. So my joyful buzz is instantly dulled, knowing that she doesn't like Kevin.

"He's fine," I reply, knowing it's not a great answer, but I also know she's going to roast me anyway. "He's been working a lot of hours so I haven't even seen him in a few days, but he texts me every morning and night. We're supposed to go out for dinner this weekend to celebrate."

Elise sighs, giving me that look that makes her normally very cute face look sort of like a sarcastic basset hound. "I'm glad, I guess. Not to beat a dead horse," —*too late*— "but you really can do better. Kevin is just so . . . meh. There's no spark, no fire between you two. It's like you're friends who fuck."

I duck my chin, not wanting her to read on my face the woeful lack of fucking that has been happening, but I'm too transparent.

"Wait . . . you two *do* fuck, right?" Elise asks, flabbergasted. "I figured that was why you were staying with him. I was sure he must be great in the sack or you'd have dumped his boring ass a long time ago."

I bite my lip, not wanting to get into this with her . . . again. But one of Elise's greatest strengths is also one of her most annoying traits as well. She's like a dog with a bone and isn't going to let this go.

"Look, he's fine," I finally reply, trying to figure out how much I need to feed Elise before she gives me a measure of peace. "He's handsome, treats me well, and when we have sex, it's good . . . I guess. I don't believe in some Prince Charming who is going to sweep me off my feet to a castle where we'll have romantic candlelit dinners, brilliant conversation, and bed-breaking sexcapades. I just want someone to share the good and bad times with, some companionship."

Elise holds back as long as she can before she explodes, her snort and guffaw of derision getting even more looks in our direction. "Then get a fucking Golden Retriever and a rabbit. The buzzing kind that uses rechargeable batteries."

One of the ladies at the next table huffs, seemingly aghast at Elise's outburst, and they stand to move toward the bar on the other side of the restaurant, far away from us. "Well, if this is the sort of trash that passes for dinner conversation," the older one says as she sticks her nose far enough into the air I wonder if it's going to be clipped by the ceiling fans, "no wonder the country's going to hell under these Millennials!"

She storms off before Elise or I can respond, but the second lady pauses slightly and talks out of the side of her mouth. "Sweetie, you do deserve more than *fine*."

With a wink, she scurries off after her friend, leaving behind a grinning Elise. "See? Even snooty old biddies know that you deserve more than *meh*."

"I know. We've had this conversation on more than one occasion, so can we drop it?" I plead between clenched teeth before calming slightly. "I want to celebrate and catch up, not argue about my love life."

Always needing the last word, Elise drops her voice, muttering under her breath. "What love life?"

"That's low."

Elise holds her hands up, and I know I've at least gotten a temporary reprieve. "Okay then, if we're sticking to work, I got a new scoop that I'm running with. I'm writing a piece about a certain famous someone who got caught sending dick pics to a social media princess. Don't ask me who because I can't divulge that yet. But it'll be all there in black and white by next week's column."

Elise is an investigative journalist, a rather fantastic one whose talents are largely being wasted on celebrity news gossip for the tabloid paper she writes for. I can't even call it a paper, really. With the downfall of actual print news, most of her stuff ends up in cyberspace, where it's digested, Tweeted, hashtagged, and churned out for the two-minute attention span types to gloat over for a moment before they move on to . . . well, whatever the next sound bite happens to be.

Every once in awhile, she'll get to do something much more newsworthy, but mostly it's fact-checking and ass-covering before the paper publishes stories celebrities would rather see disappear. I know what burns her ass even more is when she has to cover the stories where some downward-trending celebrity manufactures a scandal just to get some social media buzz going before their latest attempt at rejuvenating a career that peaked about five years ago.

This one at least sounds halfway interesting, and frankly, better than my love life, so I laugh. "Why would he send a dick pic to someone on social media? Wouldn't he assume she'd post it? What a dumbass!"

"No, it's usually close-ups and they're posted anonymously," Elise says with a snort. "Of course, she knows because she sees the user name on their direct message, but she cuts it out so that it's posted to her page as an anonymous flash of flesh. Look."

She pulls out her phone, clicking around to open an app, one I didn't design but damn sure wish I had. It's got one hell of a sweet interface, and Elise is using it to organize her web pages better than anything the normal apps have. It takes Elise only a moment to find the page she wants.

"See?" she says, showing me her phone. "People send her messages with dick pics, tit pics, whatever. If she deems them sexy enough, she posts them with little blurbs and people can comment. She also does Q-and-As with followers, shows faceless pics of herself, and gives little shows sometimes. Kinda like porn but more 'real people' instead of silicone-stuffed, pump-sucked, fake moan scenes."

She scrolls through, showing me one image after another of body part close-ups. Some of them . . . well damn, I gotta say that while they might not be professionals or anything, it's a hell of a lot hotter than anything I'm getting right now. "Wow. That's uhh . . . quite something. I don't get it, but I guess lots of folks are into it. Wait."

She stops scrolling at my near-shout, smirking. "What? See something you like?"

My mouth feels dry and my voice papery. "Go back up a couple."

She scrolls back up and I read the blurb above a collage of pics. *Little titty fuck with my new boy toy today. Look at my hungry tits and his thick cock. After this, things got a little deeper, if you know what I mean. Sorry, no pics of that, but I'll just say that he was insatiable and I definitely had a very good morning. ;)*

The pictures show a close-up of her full cleavage, a guy's dick from above, and then a few pictures of him stroking in and out of her pressed-together breasts. I'm not afraid to say the girl's got a nice rack that would probably have most of my co-workers drooling and the blood rushing from their brains to their dicks, but that's not what's causing my stomach to drop through the floor.

I know that dick.

It's the same, thick with a little curve to the right, and I can even see a sort of donut-shaped mole high on the man's thigh, right above the shaved area above the base of his cock.

Yes, that mole seals it.

That's Kevin.

His cock with another woman, fucking her for social media, thinking I'd probably never even know. He has barely touched me lately, but he's willing to do it almost publicly with some social media slut?

I realize Elise is staring at me, her previous good-natured look long gone to be replaced by an expression of concern. "Kat, are you okay? You look pale."

I point at her phone, trying my best to keep my voice level. "That post? The one right there?"

"Oh, Titty Fuck Girl?" Elise asks. "She's on here at least once a month with a new set of pics. Apparently, she loves her rack. I still think they're fake. Why?"

"She's talking about Kevin. That's him."

She gasps, turning the phone to look closer. "Holy shit, honey. Are you sure?"

I nod, tears already pooling in my eyes. "I'm sure."

She puts her phone down on the table and comes around the table to hug me. "Shit. Shit. Shit. I am so sorry. I told you that douchebag doesn't deserve someone like you. You're too fucking good for him."

I sniffle, nodding, but deep inside, I know that this is always how it goes. Every single boyfriend I've ever had ended up cheating on me. I've tried playing hard to get. I've tried being the good little go-along girlfriend. I've even tried being myself, which seems to be somewhere in between, once I figured out who I actually was.

It's even worse in bed, where I've tried being vanilla, being aggressive, and being submissive. And again, being myself, somewhere in the middle, when I figured out what I enjoyed from the experimentation.

But honestly, I've never been satisfied. No matter what, I just can't seem to find that 'sweet spot' that makes me happy and fulfilled in a relationship. And while I've tried every-thing, depending on the guy, it never works out. The boyfriends I've had, while few in number considering I can count them on one hand, all eventually cheated, saying that they just wanted something different. Something that's *not* me.

Apparently, Kevin's no different. My mood shifts wildly from self-pity to anger to finally, a numb acceptance. "What a fucking jerk. I hope he likes being a boy toy for a social media slut, because he's damn sure not my boyfriend anymore."

"That's the spirit," Elise says, refilling my wine glass. "Now, how about you and I finish off this bottle, get another, and by the time you're done, you'll have forgotten all about that loser while we take a cab back to your place?"

"Maybe I will just get a dog, and I sure as hell already have a buzzing rabbit. Several of them, in fact," I mutter. "You know what? They're better than he ever was by a damn country mile."

"Rabbits . . . they just keep going and going and going," Elise jokes, trying to keep me in good spirits. She twirls her hands in the air like the famous commercial bunny and signals for another bottle of wine.

She's right. Fuck Kevin.

GET THE FULL BOOK HERE:
mybook.to/DTalk

ABOUT THE AUTHORS

Thank you so much for reading our our cowritten novel. We hope you loved reading it as much as we loved writing it!

Want more? Join our mailing list to receive all sorts of fan extras! (If you're already on our lists, you'll get this automatically).

Willow Winters
Like her on Facebook.
View Willow's website!

Lauren Landish
Like her on Facebook.
View Lauren's website!

Check out our cowritten novels!

Highest Bidder Series

Bought
Sold
Owned
Given

Standalone Romances